About The Author

Ronald Findlay grew up in the Scottish countryside, at fifteen he left home and began his career first as a gamekeeper, later as a deer stalker and finally as a manager on a major Scottish Estate. He is a member of the Atholl Highlanders and a keen fisherman. He has also travelled extensively in Asia, South America and Europe. Ron had to give up the career he loved when he was diagnosed with Arthritis but this has led to a second career as a detective novelist. "Ghosts in the Wood" is Ron's first book featuring Stuart Brodie and Detective Ryan Jones, the first book of what Ron hopes will become a series of novels. Ron now lives in sunny California and is married with five children.

"Ghosts In The Wood"

By

Ronald Findlay

A Stuart Brodie Novel

Ghosts In The Wood is a work of fiction. Names, characters, places and incidents are the products of the Authors imagination or are used fictitiously. Any resemblance to actual events, locales or persons, living or dead, is entirely coincidental.

2007 Ronald Findlay

ISBN: 978-0-6151-7474-7

Printed in the United States of America

First Edition

www.lulu.com

This book is dedicated to my children.

Prologue

Asia Four Years Ago....

The fifth morning was like every other; hot and humid. We had a leisurely breakfast at the usual time. We were in no great hurry to get where we were going and we didn't want to raise any suspicion by changing our routine. It was to be a daylight strike, in the jungle this was the wise thing to do.

Russell told me to leave all personal effects behind especially anything that could identify me. The previous day we told everyone we met that we were intending to visit the Waterfalls. The Waterfalls were a major tourist attraction situated six miles north of the town.

When we arrived at the falls Russell parked the car in the area he had chosen two days previous. After changing into light-weight fatigues we set off on our four mile trek into the jungle.

The drug smugglers' camp was in a remote part of jungle on the other side of the border. It was swelteringly hot and clammy our clothes clung to our bodies saturated with sweat. Russell had given me some drops earlier to prevent my eyes stinging.

"You can't afford to lose your vision in a situation like this" he had told me.

We were both equipped with .44 automatic pistols and pump action shotguns, the type the police and military use. They were loaded with eight double-o buck shot cartridges that could stop an elephant at close range, let alone a man.

Fifty feet from the make shift camp we could see men sitting round a camp fire, talking and smoking. The strong smell of cannabis and of boiling rice lingered in the still, humid air. We waited for ten minutes in a crouched position checking if there was anyone else in the vicinity. Those ten minutes seemed like an hour. My role was to cover Russell's back.

Russell made a gesture with his hand holding out three fingers, indicating that there were three men. His next indication was with an open hand the sign for me to stay put.

As quick as a flash, Russell darted forward low as he went, with his shotgun at the ready. The adrenalin was now raging through my body I felt like charging after him, but I managed to restrain myself. Realizing what was about to happen, the three men started shouting as they reached for their guns. A second later, all hell let loose as Russell's shotgun shattered the silence, sounding like muffled thunder due to the density of the jungle.

At the same time I heard voices from behind me: two men. I crouched and spun round, as bullets flew just over my head, the men behind had spotted me. With no time to take cover my survival instinct took over. I let blast with the shotgun hitting the nearest gunman squarely in the chest. The shot threw him backwards knocking his colleague behind off balance, before the second gunman regained his footing I shot him in his head which exploded in all directions. The headless body took a few steps forward still clutching his AK 47, before slumping to the ground in a heap.

Silence, it was all over, well almost. The three men that had been sitting at the camp fire were now lifeless, blood and parts of their innards were splattered everywhere. Russell took out his hand gun and shot each of them in the head, he told me to do the same. I did as he asked for I felt no remorse whatsoever after all they had tried to kill me. I only had to shoot one, though, as the other no longer had a head. After the deed was done I asked Russell.

"Why shoot them in the head when it's quite obvious

they're dead?"

"Two reasons my friend first it's always wise to make sure that the target is dead, second it's a clear indication that it was an execution. A stern warning to others, not that they give a shit. You seemed to handle that rather well quite a natural I would say, how do you feel about it?"

"I feel quite good actually, though I did feel a bit apprehensive when the bullets started flying right enough"

"That's not a bad thing it keeps you on your toes"

Before making our hasty retreat we destroyed the heroin.

1

It was five thirty on a mild but damp, late summer
morning. The sun was just beginning to burn through the
haze which swirled around the hills and lay in the glens.
There was little sign of life, just Stuart Brodie, the deer
stalker, out early, happily unaware that his past was about to
catch up with him.

'Not long now' thought Stuart as the Land Rover
crawled up the track towards the West Crag, Stuart's
favourite viewing spot. From here he could spy for miles in
all directions and with luck, pick out a few beasts.

Stuart pulled-in stopping under an overhanging crag
overlooking a two hundred foot, sheer drop. He switched
off the engine, rolled down the window, stuck out his head
and felt the cool autumn-scented breeze on his face. The
wind was coming from the west, just as he had anticipated.
Time for a quick cup of coffee, giving any deer disturbed by
the Land Rovers' engine a chance to settle.

Slipping out of the Land Rover, Stuart closed the door
without making a sound. He made his way along the side
of the crag. Keeping low and through force of habit,
checking the ground before each step. Reaching he
destination, Stuart squatted behind a rock scanning the basin
shaped area. A closer look through the binoculars revealed
a group of deer five hinds and two calves.

Somewhere in the distance Stuart heard the call of the
Golden Plover, the countryside alarm, alerting all that a
predator was afoot. Scanning carefully, Stuart caught a

glimpse of something red moving along the edge of a peat bog. A fox was heading home to the other side of the basin to a cairn, a well-known den for holding cubs each year. The dog fox will lie up close to his cubs protecting them and providing for them. Likely, as not he had just caught a tasty meal for his children.

Stuart slipped the Mannlicher .270 out of its cover, checked the barrel for blockages and slipped the bolt into position, making sure the action was running smoothly He peered over the top of the rock. Straight in front of him, about a hundred yards away, a large hind was sitting, facing his way, her head slightly tilted backwards, her bottom jaw in contented motion, her eyes partially closed. Three more hinds and two calves were just to her left. The fifth hind sat below the group. All that was visible of this hind were her ears, but that was okay as Stuart knew that she would probably stand after the first shot went off.

Stuart slid backwards a length and put in his earplugs, raised and lowered the rifle bolt, slipped the safety catch off, popped up the lens caps and eased himself forward. He looked through the scope and positioned the cross hairs on the neck of the first hind just below the jaw. He gently squeezed the trigger and crack went the rifle.

Quickly reloading, the cross-hairs already on the second neck and crack, number two fell down. All of the other deer were now rising to their feet, the furthest away had already risen, turned and was for the off. The cross-hairs quickly found the spot at the base of her skull, crack. No time to watch her crumple to the ground as the rest were beginning scatter. One hind had bolted off to the left the other was over the rise and temporarily out of sight. The two calves had stopped sixty yards to the right, they would not go far. Stuart swiftly moved to a crouching position, leaned over and in one gentle movement, swung the rifle onto the fleeing deer. He found the spot and squeezed the trigger.

The bullet struck home, the hind stumbled and fell into a forward summersault.

Stuart reloaded and changed the now empty clip for a full one. The two calves were still standing together seemingly mesmerized, but that was short-lived as two more reports come from the .270.

The last hind had now reached the edge of the basin. She stopped and looked back towards him, broadside-on, about five hundred yards away. Stuart repositioned himself on the rock and took aim, placing the cross-hairs just below the shoulder, allowing for a slight drop in the bullet at that distance. Almost simultaneously after the crack from the rifle, there was the dull whack as the bullet struck home. The beast fell to the ground, lifeless - killing was what Stuart did best

Back at the Land Rover, Stuart took his mobile phone from the rucksack and switched it on. One missed call. Stuart listened to the message. It was from the Factor.

"Call me as soon as possible. It's very urgent." The Factor sounded stressed.

"Later." said Stuart out loud. He then poured himself a cup of coffee and started on some sandwiches. Little did he know that this call would involve Stuart in a murder investigation and lead to a confrontation with the most dangerous man Stuart had ever known.

2

Stuart often envied the Factor's job, sitting in a comfy, warm office all day, from nine to five managing the estate's affairs, albeit, there was probably a lot more to it than that.

On the estate there were five tenanted farms and over two hundred rented houses. There was a lot of work involved with the maintenance of properties, not to mention managing the ever disgruntled occupants. Stuart always came to the same conclusion, in that he was happier, maybe not so well off, but happier out in the woods or the hills as opposed to sitting in a nice warm office all day.

With a sigh, Stuart pressed the Factor's number. It rang out a few times before being answered.

"Hello Peter, Stuart here."

"Where the hell have you been? I have been trying to get hold of you all morning." said the Factor. He sounded both annoyed and worried.

"Out on the hill at Achrean"

"Well you might at least answer your bloody phone."

"You don't honestly think I carry my mobile switched on when I'm stalking do you? Only an idiot would do that." said Stuart in calm tone, as he wouldn't stand for any shit from anyone, no matter who they were.

"Okay" conceded the Factor. "But listen, D.S. Jones of North London C.I.D., has been asking all sorts of questions about you and wants you to call him as soon as you can. What is going on Stuart?"

"What sort of questions?" "Questions such as; how long have you been working on the estate? Where you live? What you do? Where you go and who you see? Look Stuart, if there is something I should know about, you better tell me. This seems quite serious. Come and see me at the office as soon as you can. It's time we caught up with things anyway."

"Yeah Ok Peter, I will. I'll come tomorrow morning. Bye for now." Stuart switched off his phone.

"Shit!" said Stuart aloud. This was all he needed. Four years he had been back on the estate surely this was all behind him.

Stuart had left school at the age of fifteen and over the years had worked on various estates around Scotland. He had been working in this job for six years and then drastically, his whole life had changed. His wife had left him, taking the kids. Maybe the marriage hadn't been perfect, but it had suited Stuart, and losing the kids, well that had broken Stuart's heart. Then he received an invitation to visit a friend in Asia.

It came just at the right time for Stuart, he needed to get away. Stuart resigned from his job and sold most of his possessions. What he didn't sell he simply gave away. Stuart went to Asia, initially for a four-week visit, which ended up stretching to three years.

During the time Stuart spent in Asia, he learnt a lot about himself, he realised what type of person he really was. Stuart participated in things that he never knew he was capable of. Maybe it had been the company that he got in tow with, or maybe it was the excitement and the thrill of danger that had drawn Stuart into the new world.

Then things started to turn bad, about as bad as they could possibly get. So, Stuart came home to resume his position on the estate. For the past four years, Stuart had never mentioned to anyone about the years he had spent in

Asia, other than that he had enjoyed himself. Nor had he heard from anyone from the past.

Why now after all this time. What had happened? Had the police found out about his exploits in Asia? Stuart contemplated taking off somewhere, but he couldn't face running again. If they were onto him, he would see it through.

The roar of the engine broke Stuart's train of thought. The estate handyman and Stuart's helper, young Steve had arrived in the Argocat, laden with dead deer.

3

D.S. Ryan Jones and his junior partner D.C. Chris
Black checked into the Braes of Brackie Hotel. The hotel
was around forty miles north of Glasgow, located in a small
village by the sea. It had been built during the Victorian
period in the style of a medieval castle.

The views from the hotel were quite breathtaking in
all directions. Looking to one side was the sea and the
distant islands, looking inland gave to a marvellous view of
the towering mountains. The air was clean, no petrol fumes,
just bracing, crisp air.

Inside the hotel, most of the original features
remained. The wooden floors were worn and discoloured in
places, due to the thousands of feet that had trodden them
over the years. The walls had fine oak panelling. Gracing
the walls of the hallways and dining room, hung ancient oil
paintings which depicted hunting and landscape scenes.
There were antique swords and rows of stuffed animal
heads, retaining the feel of a bygone era. From the large
windows, hung thick velvet curtains that draped all the way
to the floor.

A grand place indeed, thought Ryan Jones, feeling he
had stepped back in time. This was the second time Ryan
had been up to Scotland; the first time was for the same
reason – murder. That murder inquiry had turned out to be

fruitless, Ryan was hoping for a better result this time. Ryan was forty four years old. He had been born in Wales, but grew up in the north of London. He was five foot ten in height with a stocky muscular build. He looked and was very capable of handling himself.

He had started his working career at sixteen on a building site, as a labourer, where he developed his muscular physique. At the age of twenty, Ryan joined the police force, did well enough to get into the C.I.D. and worked his way up to become sergeant. He had little interest in further promotion; being stuck behind an office desk did not appeal to him.

Ryan liked getting out and about where he could put his talent to use. He prided himself on being able to tell if someone was lying, or if something was just not quite right, relying on his intuition. He was from the old school, a first class detective.

Ryan's wife had died of cancer five years ago. He had a twenty-five year old daughter, Clare she was married to Grant Collins, a very successful civil engineer. Just over a year ago Grant was head-hunted by an international company and was made an offer that he couldn't refuse. Unfortunately, his new position was in Canada. Ryan was unhappy about this but there was nothing he could do but wish them well. He and Clare called each other twice a week and now with Clare expecting her first child, Ryan was looking forward to becoming a grandfather. He was also looking forward to his Easter holiday, for that's when he planned to go and visit. Ryan had not re-married and he had no intention of ever doing so.

Ryan enjoyed the pace of life in Scotland so different to that of the south of England, a lot less hustle and bustle. He knew there was a lot of crime in Glasgow but even so, compared to London everything seemed so much more relaxed. The people seemed friendly, although he had difficulty understanding the way some of them spoke, especially the ones with broad Glaswegian accents. Ryan had noticed almost straight away, how the air was so much cleaner and fresher, than London where some days he struggled for breath. Maybe he should ask for a transfer? He needed a change.

Ryan was in Scotland as part of an investigation into four murders which had taken place in London. The murder victims were known drug-dealers and linked to a massive drug ring at large in the U.K. The drug ring was suspected to have a strong Scottish connection, but the Drug Squad had few leads.

Ryan following a hunch made the trip to Scotland to search a Glasgow flat owned by one of the victims. During the search Ryan found a notebook containing a familiar name, a name that had kept cropping up in the investigation down south, 'Stuart Brodie'. The scribbled inscription had read: "One hundred thousand pounds in cash to be handed to Stuart Brodie." There had been no mention of when or where the money was to be handed over. Ryan wanted to determine if the money was payment for Brodie's part in the drug ring or even in the murders? As to where the money was now, Ryan had no idea, for the money was not in Stuart Brodie's bank account. All that Brodie had in his account was five and a half thousand pounds. But since the inquiries in Glasgow and London were grinding to a halt, Stuart Brodie was all he had to go on.

When D.S. Ryan Jones had spoken briefly to the Factor on the telephone inquiring about Stuart Brodie, the Factor had mentioned that Stuart Brodie stayed at the Braes of Brackie Hotel from time to time. So, Ryan had decided to go there and check the place out. On making enquires at the reception, much to his surprise and good luck, Ryan discovered that Stuart Brodie was actually staying at the hotel

That was a bit of luck and added to Ryan's positive state of mind. Okay, maybe having drug dealers killed, up and down the country, might be good for society, but murder was murder and if Stuart Brodie was involved, then Ryan would have him.

4

Stuart parked the land rover in its usual place, near to the back door of the hotel. He thought this gave a little added security.

Stuart stayed at the Braes of Brackie Hotel when he was over on this part of the estate which had been twice a week for the last three months, at the Estates' expense of course.

The Factor had first suggested putting a caravan on the hill for him to stay in, nice and handy for an early start he had said. Stuart had soon told him what he thought of that idea; yes, nice and handy indeed, but after being out on the hill all day, usually soaked to the skin, the first thing that he wanted was a hot bath, or at least a shower and somewhere to dry your clothes.

Stuart went in the back door through the hall to Reception.

"Hello Stuart." said the woman behind the reception desk giving him her best smile. The woman's name was Sharon. She was reasonably attractive, in her early thirties, about five ten in height, with shoulder length blonde hair. Dyed mused Stuart, as she had very dark eyebrows, she seemed a bit on the thin side. Stuart thought having small breasts gave that impression. Sharon always looked immaculately dressed and today she was wearing a pale blue silk blouse and a black pencil style skirt. Her hands were elegant, with well-manicured nails painted in the same colour as her lipstick, a pale red. She still wore her wedding rings. The only other make-up was light blue eye-shadow that high-lighted her ice-blue eyes. Stuart often wondered why she stayed in a remote area like this, when she could be in a big city with all the other glamorous women, in a high profile job for she seemed both intelligent and well-educated. Perhaps, it is the love for her dead husband that is keeping her here thought Stuart. Sharon's husband was killed in a fishing accident two years ago, leaving her to bring up their two young children on her own. Was there another man in her life? Stuart had never asked.

"Hello Sharon. How are you today?" enquired Stuart, returning her smile.

"Fine thanks. Have you had a good day murdering little bambies?" Sharon's tone was flirtatious rather than combative.

"Great, but I didn't kill too many. I left a few to grow a bit until next week."

"You're a wicked man Stuart Brodie. I suppose you want the gun room keys?" Sharon placed them and his room key on the desk.

"Thank you very much Sharon." said Stuart giving her a wink. He picked up the keys and turned to walk away.

"Have a nice night." Sharon called after him in a sweet girlish voice.

Stuart stopped and turned round to see her smiling face.

"What time do you finish tonight?" asked Stuart.

"Why?" Sharon's eyes twinkled, a twinkle that Stuart had not picked up on before.

"Would you like to have a drink with me later?"

"I'll see if I can get a baby sitter."

"Ok, I will be in the lounge if you can." said Stuart. He then turned and walked towards the gun room thinking;

Damn why did I do that? Already wishing he hadn't asked her.

After a much-needed shower and shave, Stuart pulled on his Levis and put on a black shirt that he had brought with him. He brushed his hair but did not bother to look in the mirror, as he knew what the reflection would be: a once-handsome man getting old, with greying hair and lines, not through laughter, but from hard living.

Stuart walked into the hotel restaurant and was greeted by the waitress Karen with a friendly smile. Karen was a small dark- haired girl about twenty years old with a rotund figure. Karen was a bit shy, but her manner was very pleasant.

"Would you like to see the menu Mr Brodie?" said Karen after showing Stuart to a seat by the window.

"No thanks Karen, I will have the soup and a fillet steak with chips please"

"And what would you like to drink sir?"

"I think a bottle of merlot thanks."

"Thank you sir." said Karen and she headed off towards the kitchen.

Stuart glanced around the restaurant. It was quite busy with mainly elderly couples, apart from the two men sitting in a far corner. They were clean-cut, dressed in casuals and looked about the same age as himself in their early to mid forties. One of them was looking directly at Stuart. Stuart caught his eye as he turned to the other, speaking very softly so no one would hear him. But Stuart could hear in his own way. He had learned to lip-read years ago when he lived abroad, watching dubbed television for hours at a time.

"So that's what Stuart Brodie looks like." said D.C Black. "Shall we go over?"

"No let's wait until he has finished his dinner." replied Ryan Jones.

"He looks a hard bastard right enough Sarge" observed Black.

Fucking Hell, thought Stuart after the initial shock .Who the fuck were they? He said 'Sarge' so, they were policemen, thought Stuart, but what did they want with him? Stuart remained his cool self, turned and stared out of the window, his brain desperately searching for answers. Peter had told him that the C.I.D. from London wanted to speak to him. Peter had not said they were here in Scotland! Maybe Peter didn't know they were here. Maybe they were not from London. There was one way to find out. Stuart got up from the table and headed for reception. If they had checked in, Sharon would tell him who they were.

Stuart arrived back at his table, at the same time as Karen got there with his soup. The open bottle of merlot was already on the table with a full glass next to it. Stuart thanked Karen and started on his soup, gazing abstractly around the dining room, as people do when they are on their own, pausing long enough on the two C.I.D. men, to make out what the larger of the two was saying about him.

"Who the fuck does he think he is? Lord of the fucking manor?"

'That's right dick-head, so you better be careful what you say' Stuart though to himself. Stuart felt a bit more at ease now that he knew who they were. Why had they tracked him down? It must be pretty important, he thought.

Stuart finished his meal, picked up the three-quarter full bottle of merlot and headed through to the lounge. He sat on one of the leather couches next to the open fire, thinking to himself 'this is as good a place as any for a confrontation.'

5

The two policemen walked over to Stuart with their pints of beer.

"Mind if we join you? That's a rather inviting fire." said D.S. Jones.

"Not at all Sergeant Jones" replied Stuart. Stuart looked to the other man. "I am sorry, but I have forgotten your name already" said Stuart with exaggerated politeness.

The two C.I.D. officers looked at each other with uneasy surprise. So he knows who we are? So much for the element of surprise, thought D.S. Jones.

Stuart motioned with his hand for them to sit down.

"You obviously know who I am, so I checked out who you were. And yes, I am treated here like the lord of the fucking manner."

The two policemen gave each other wary looks. There was silence for about a minute.

"But how?" started D.C. Black. He was cut off by Jones "He can lip read you bloody fool."

"Oh shit!"

"So what can I do for you?" said Stuart not really wanting to know.

"Well as you already know, I am D.S. Ryan Jones and this is D.C. Chris Black. We would like to ask you some questions about your time in Asia and the people that you met."

"Why? It's been over four years since I was in Asia"

"We just want you to tell us who you met and spoke to when you were there that is all." "I would like to know why first." insisted Stuart.

"We are not at liberty to discuss that at the moment"

Fuck thought Stuart did policemen really say 'at liberty to discuss', were they really that pompous? But he buttoned his lip and said repressively "When you are let me know, then I will speak to you."

The heat from the fire and Stuart's attitude was starting to irritate the policemen. "Look Stuart, we have come a long way to speak to you and we were hoping that you would co-operate with us." said Jones.

Jones weighed things up; this was a smart guy, not some simple country bumpkin as their prejudices had led them to believe. Should we tell him at least part of the reason why we need to speak to him and hopefully get his co-operation? Or should we make it official and take him to the nearest police station for questioning and try to get information out of him that way? The problem was Stuart would probably clam up altogether. Jones could not afford for that to happen, after all, he was the only lead they had to go on. Jones looked towards Chris Black. "What do you think Chris?"

"I think we should take him to the nearest station with a cell and keep him there overnight. He might be more willing to talk to us in the morning."

"Fine by me." said Stuart as he started to rise from the couch.

"Sit down." said Jones rather sharply. "Chris, go and get us another drink and one for Stuart."

"No thanks, I am quite happy with my wine." replied Stuart. Chris reluctantly got up and slouched off towards the bar.

"My colleague is right you know, we could take you in, but I don't think it would do any good, so I am going to tell you what this is all about."

"When you were in Asia, a person by the name of Richard, or Rick Maynard, the name you probably knew him by, was murdered. We don't suspect you of the murder, although we know you were a suspect at the time. You were arrested after Rick's girlfriend went to the police accusing you. The guy that bailed you out of jail was Russell Hodges. You then you did a runner and came back to Scotland. Correct so far?"

"Go on" said Stuart his eyes locked with Jones. Neither of them wanted to be the first to drop their gaze.

"About a week after you left the country, three more people were killed, two of them were known associates of Rick Maynard, and the other one was a cousin of Russell Hodges: David Philips. You knew him" it wasn't a question but Stuart nodded briefly.

"We think you probably knew them or knew of them. Then Russell Hodges was arrested for the murder of Maynard's associates. His motive was retaliation for his cousin's death. Hodges spent two years in jail. Then he somehow manages to get bail and has not been seen or heard of since. But in the last few months, we have had four murders in North London, all linked to the late Rick Maynard. The victims were all involved in the drug trade. The drug squad have been trying to get a fix on this gang for years. We even had one of them in custody for a while, but we never had enough evidence to convict him unlucky for him, because he was one of the murder victims. Now it seems like some vigilante is out for revenge, Hodges we think. We are up in Scotland because the most recent victim came from Glasgow. We know that there is a Scottish connection to the drug-ring. In fact we suspect that the drugs are coming into the UK via Scotland's west coast, but we don't know where or how. Anyway, while conducting our inquiries in Glasgow, guess what name crops up again? Just as it had in London so we thought it was time we looked you up. We are not accusing you of anything Stuart; we just want to know about anyone you met through Maynard in Asia or in the U.K. And of course we want to know all about your friend Russell Hodges. So will you speak to us?"

Just then a huge figure appeared next to their table. "Hello Stuart." said Steve while nodding to Jones as an extension of the same greeting. "Can I get you a pint?"

Stuart paused for a moment, saved by the bell. Steve's arrival would give him time to think. "Yes please Steve, I will have a pint of Guinness. This is Ryan Jones from London, up here doing a bit of business."

Steve and Ryan shook hands and exchanged a polite greeting. Steve asked him if he could get him a drink, but the policeman declined saying that his friend Chris was getting him one. Steve turned and went to the bar.

"What is your answer Stuart?" prodded Jones.

"Yes okay, but tomorrow."

"Fine, shall we say after breakfast?"

"Fine by me"

Jones stood up just as Chris arrived back with their drinks. He and Chris moved to a table on the other side of the lounge. Stuart was deep in thought when laughter from the direction of the bar caught his attention. Standing at the bar next to Steve, sharing some joke or other was Sharon. Damn! Stuart thought, he had completely forgotten about her.

6

Stuart awoke late the next morning, alone with the lingering sweet smell of Sharon. She had slipped away during the night back to her children. Stuart lay in bed for a bit feeling totally relaxed. It had been the best sleep he had had in a long time. He let the pleasant thoughts of the night before drift in his mind, was it to be just a casual one night stand of lust? Or was there some chemistry pulling them together?

During breakfast Stuart had decided that if D.S. Jones wanted to speak to him, then he would have to come to his house. He didn't like the feeling of being tracked down and was uneasy at the hotel.

There had not been any sign of Jones nor his side-kick at breakfast. Stuart decided that he would leave a message at reception for them. To Stuart's surprise, he was told at reception that the two policemen had checked out first thing, and they had left a message for him.

The note left by Jones read:

"Sorry unable to talk with you today, something urgent has came up, but please call me tomorrow, my mobile number is (07723958204)."

It was signed Ryan Jones. Stuart felt relieved. He got in the land rover ready for the drive to the estate office and his appointment with the Factor. As Stuart was leaving the village, he drove past Sharon's house. He contemplated popping in but soon dismissed the thought. It was not the right time to start a relationship. But when would it be, if ever? Stuart had not had a serious relationship since his wife had left him. Once bitten, twice shy.

On the drive Stuart went back over what had happened in Asia.

Stuart first met Rick Maynard in one of the bars at Heathrow airport. They had shared the same table. Over a few beers, Rick told Stuart all about Asia, Rick was very knowledgeable about Asian countries, having lived in Asia for several years. Stuart enjoyed listening to Rick's stories, and they had agreed to meet at the end of the flight.

At the time Stuart thought meeting Rick Maynard was a piece of good luck, but Rick turned out to be Stuart's biggest nightmare. Over the months Rick gained Stuart's confidence and started asking him for favours, to bring money from London. Rick told Stuart that the money was to invest in properties.

Then Stuart met another friend Russell Hodges, also in a bar. Thinking back Stuart now knows that Russell probably sought him out because of Stuart's connection with Rick. After establishing a friendly acquaintance with Stuart, Russell carefully informed him that Rick was in fact a drug dealer. Stuart didn't appreciate being used, put in danger and lied to especially not by a drug dealer. That put an end to Stuart and Rick's friendship, although the consequences did not end there.

Meanwhile, Russell and Stuart became very good friends. Having a common interest in shooting, Russell took Stuart to a local shooting range, where he taught Stuart how to use a handgun. Russell was an expert. Russell used a .44 semi automatic and could group all the rounds within the bull's eye. This impressed Stuart. He found out through their long conversations, that Russell had gained his expertise while serving in the army.

On one occasion, Stuart commented that he preferred rifles.

"Well, let us put you to the test." Russell had replied. The only rifles they had at the shooting range were .22 Rim fires. The rifle range was short, only fifty yards, but with open sights it was long enough. It had been Russell's turn to be impressed, for not only did Stuart put all of the ten rounds in the bull; eight of them had gone through the same hole in the centre of the bull.

As Stuart and Russell's friendship deepened, they began taking trips to other parts of the country, seeing the sights, drinking having fun sometimes joined by the murdered David, Russell's cousin and of course there were always lots of beautiful young ladies. It was during one of these trips that Stuart realised what Russell was really up to.

Was Russell now in London? Although Jones had not revealed the names of the four men killed, Stuart had an idea who they might be and he also knew that if it was Russell committing the murders, then there could well be a lot more. Russell Hodges was a professional killer who enjoyed his work, was ruthless and a very dangerous man. God help anyone who's on his list.

7

Stuart arrived at the estate office by mid-morning. The Factor's Range Rover was parked in its usual spot. The Factor was about the same age as Stuart, in his mid-forties. He had a very straight stature and was of medium build. Although his blond hair was now starting to recede, he was still an attractive man and very much the gentleman.

Peter Grant, the Factor, came from a wealthy family who owned an estate on the Isle of Mull. Sadly for him he had not inherited the estate, as his father had divorced his mother and remarried. The woman he married had two sons from a previous marriage and somehow she had managed to get Peter's father to change his will, cutting Peter out of it all together.

Now, though, not only was Peter the Factor of this prestigious estate, he was also the owner of a large farm and several other properties. He had married well, to a wealthy woman and they had two sons. He was doing alright for himself, thought Stuart.

Stuart pushed open the heavy oak door. Christine, the estate secretary, was seated at her desk typing. She looked up as Stuart entered the room, peering over the top of her horn-rimmed glasses, looking as miserable as ever. Appearances however can be deceiving, for she was actually a very pleasant woman.

Christine's hair had turned white with age; she could have retired ten years ago. She was a spinster with no family whatsoever. This was her life. Fifty years she had worked in the estate office. If there was anything that you wanted to know about the estate, or people that once worked or lived on it, Christine could tell off the top of her head. She might be old, but all the lights were still on.

"Hello Stuart, how are you?"

"Very well thanks and you?"

"Oh I am fine. Are you here to see Peter?"

"Yes."

"I will let him know you are here" Christine picked up the phone, spoke to the Factor and told Stuart to go right in.

"Thanks Christine." said Stuart giving her a smile.

Stuart walked along the old flagstone corridor which led to the Factor's office. The building had once been a coach house, many years ago when the estate had been a stately home, in all its grandeur and glory. But sadly over the years, large chunks of the estate had been sold off, mainly to corporate groups, the ones with large amounts of money to invest, or as some people suggested money to hide from the tax man.

The estate had changed hands a few years ago, after the previous owner had died and the estate inherited by a distant relative. The present owners very rarely visited. They spent most of their time in Switzerland or Italy, leaving the Factor in charge of running the estate.

Stuart knocked at the door and walked in. The office was in the style of a Victorian study, with large oak book cases. The wooden floor was well-polished and creaked as you walked over it. In the centre was a large oriental rug that was threadbare in places. It was probably over a hundred years old. The Factor made a gesture with his hand towards the seat in front of his large oak desk.

"How are you Stuart?"

"Fine thanks." replied Stuart as he made himself comfortable in the large leather chair.

"So how did you get on this week?"

"Fine, that's another fifteen less deer to worry about, but I must have seen at least another fifty or so and I still haven't been near the big wood on the far side of the hill yet. God only knows how many could be in there."

"Maybe you need to spend a bit more time over on the West Coast. Now what do the police from London want with you?" said the Factor changing the subject or perhaps getting to the point.

"Nothing really, it just so happens that someone I knew when I was abroad has been killed. They asked me if I knew any of his friends or contacts, that sort of thing, you know, but like I told them, I only met this guy once or twice. Speaking of which, I met these cops last night at the hotel. They said they were in Glasgow on business and it was just coincidence that they met me" said Stuart in such a way that he didn't give the Factor any indication of his real concern.

"Okay if you are sure that's all it is. Anyway, I think that you should concentrate on getting rid of as many deer as you can just now. Forget about the rest of the estate for the time being. And let me know, whatever the news or the outcome is with the police from London, Okay?" said the Factor as he got up from his chair.

This was Stuart's cue to leave. A busy man, thought Stuart. Peter was a good boss to Stuart, for he never interfered, let him do his own thing so long as he got results, which he did. In fact Stuart had quite a lot of respect for the Factor.

It had been the Factor's suggestion that Stuart take off somewhere for a year or two, after his marriage break-up. And the Factor had stuck to his word by saying there would always be a job for Stuart on the estate.

Still, Stuart left the office feeling uneasy, it was bad enough that his past had caught up with him; he definitely didn't want the Factor to know about it. Stuart chatted to

Christine for a few minutes before leaving the building.
Then he headed to his cottage.

8

The cottage that Stuart lived in was situated nine miles south of the estate office. It was situated well off the main road, standing on its own, in a very secluded area surrounded by large pine trees. There were no other houses within a five mile radius. With the cottage being so secluded, it gave total peace and quiet, just the way Stuart liked it.

The cottage itself dated back to the nineteenth century. The structure was still original, although the interior had been modernised about ten years ago, when oil-fired central heating had been installed. The cottage consisted of two bedrooms, a sitting room, kitchen and bathroom. The rooms themselves were quite small, but it was all Stuart needed living on his own. Stuart's children very rarely visited, for they now lived in Cornwall with their mother, who had remarried. They did however keep in touch.

The spare bedroom was used as a gun room. It had two steel cabinets that were bolted to the wall and floor. There were bars on the window. It also had a solid wooden door that was steel-lined, with three separate locks. It was a very secure room. The other rooms were sparsely furnished but comfortable. Stuart did not see the need to waste money on lavish things.

Outside, the garden had become overgrown with weeds. He planned to tidy it up some weekend but never got round to it. The little time that Stuart spent at the cottage, he preferred just sitting back with a good book. Besides, he rather liked the natural, wild state the garden was in. Not far from the cottage, there was a small stream with crystal clear water. Flowing steadily, the stream originated at a nearby hill loch and weaved its way down through the hills and woods. The stream provided the water supply to the cottage. In the stream there was an abundance of brown trout, some of which were of a reasonable size. Stuart would often sit by a large pool watching the trout, tempted to get his fly rod and try to catch a few, but he never did.

While sitting on the bank watching the trout as they rose to the surface, feeding on flies, Stuart always thought back to his youth, when he had so desperately tried to catch a large trout. This particular trout lived in a large pool.   It was always sitting in the same spot, just waiting to be caught, or so Stuart used to think. Try as hard as he might, Stuart never did.   He used every type of bait that he could think of, but to no avail.

Then one summer morning, Stuart arrived with all his various baits, thinking to himself, this is the day. He had crept up to the edge of the pool as he always did, expecting to see the large trout sitting in its usual spot. Stuart had been totally shocked at the sight that lay before him.

The big trout was there alright, along with dozens of others. They were all dead, floating belly-up on the surface, large and small. Stuart couldn't believe his eyes.   He sat for ages staring at the massacre, stunned. Who or what could have done such a thing?

Stuart found out later that day that poachers had poisoned the water further up the river. They had thrown a tin of Cymag into the water, which deoxygenates it, killing every fish in the water downstream for almost half a mile. This had sickened Stuart so much that he never fished again for almost ten years. Even now Stuart preferred just to watch them.

9

Too many coincidences, thought Stuart as he woke up to a bright, sunny morning.

Thoughts had been playing on his mind all night. How did the police know where he was staying? Either they had followed him, or someone had told them. The only person Stuart knew that they had spoken to about him, was the Factor.

The Factor was the type of person who would not divulge other people's business, unless for a very good reason. With the police being involved, maybe he thought he had reason enough.

In Stuart's mind, the Factor had seemed over-keen to find out what the police wanted.

Another thing, what made the police so sure that Russell was behind the killings? Stuart thought hard. Maybe he, Stuart was a suspect? Maybe he was being set up? Jones did say that his name kept coming up, although he did not say how.

Stuart suspected that behind it all, there was the drug dealing and a professional killer out for retribution. Stuart thought he had left that all far behind him in Asia he desperately wanted to let sleeping dogs lie. Unfortunately, the dogs seemed to be wakening up.

After a good hearty breakfast, Stuart went for a long walk along by the loch. He wanted to clear his head and rid it of the unpleasant thoughts and focus on his best course of action. Stuart thought back to the first mission he went on with Russell. Stuart had felt excited, until the bullets started to fly. Then a sudden fear had set in. For up to that point was just like deer-stalking back in Scotland, only now their quarry was shooting back.

At the far side of the loch, where the water was shallow, a Grey Heron stood motionless on one leg. The Heron slowly straightened its long neck, turning its head towards a nearby reed bed. Something had the Heron's attention, disturbing its morning nap. Stuart concentrated his gaze on the reed bed, searching for whatever it was that had disturbed the Heron. Was he being watched? There was the slightest of movements in the reed bed. A spindly willow branch shuddered every few seconds. Then Stuart realised it was a roe deer marking his territory.

Stuart knew he was becoming paranoid, possibly with good reason. He decided the only thing to do was to co-operate with D.S. Jones, Russell was simply too dangerous.

Back at the cottage, Stuart dialled the number.
"Hello D.S. Jones speaking."
"Hi, Stuart Brodie here, you asked me to give you a call." said Stuart, hoping he was doing the right thing.
"Thanks for calling me Stuart. I am going to be in Glasgow over the weekend but if it is okay with you, I would like to meet with you, say maybe Monday or Tuesday. If I give you a call the night before, then perhaps you could let me know where you will be and I will come and meet you. Is that okay with you Stuart?"
"Sure, that will be fine. I will probably be back where we met last night, but still phone me just in case I am not." said Stuart.

They exchanged goodbyes and Stuart switched off his mobile.

If they weren't going to meet until Monday or Tuesday night, this would give Stuart the weekend to think

Ghosts In The Wood

things over. Things like, could he trust Jones and just how much information to give him?   Not much choice, he thought if he wanted to see an end to the predicament he was in.

45

10

The weather had changed for the worse during the course of the weekend. It was now a very wet miserable Monday morning. Stuart took his time driving as the road conditions were not good. Stuart eventually arrived back at the Braes of Brackie Hotel. He would check himself in for the week, and then head out to the wood on a stalk.

Sharon was on reception, and kept him chatting for quite some time. Stuart felt a familiar unease; he didn't want to get involved and was worried Sharon might be taking their brief fling too seriously.

"By the way the Factor called earlier to let us know you were on your way over and he asked if D.S. Jones was booked into the hotel." Sharon dropped this into conversation just as Stuart turned to leave.

"Odd" thought Stuart "Why was Peter so concerned?"

"Maybe I should have told him about Asia, but I can't jeopardize my position on the estate. I will just have to hope that the Factor will understand if he ever finds out the truth. I'll go with the flow for the time being, hope the police finish asking questions, head back to London and out of my life."

Stuart drove to the wood, got out of the Land Rover and headed up one of the forest tracks, checking as he went for any signs of deer. There appeared to be signs of deer everywhere, but not much sign of anything else. The wood in fact was ghostly quiet, apart from the shrill call of a buzzard somewhere in the distance. Stuart had seen very few deer in the wood. He put this down to the wind, which seemed to swirl wherever there was an opening in the trees, casting his scent in every direction, warning the deer of his presence well in advance, this was going to be a very difficult wood to stalk deer.

Stuart walked the entire top edge of the wood, taking note of where the most used tracks were that led from the wood onto the hill. By doing this, it not only gave him an indication as to the density of the deer population. After reaching the highest point of the hill, but still having a view of the wood, Stuart sat down and surveyed the scene before him.

Beyond the wood he could see for miles. Looking out across the sea towards the rugged islands, the view was quite spectacular. The rain had completely stopped, giving way to a clear blue sky with hardly a cloud in sight. The wind had dropped to a slight breeze. As there was still a pleasant warmth in the late afternoon sun, Stuart absorbed the heat, letting his mind go blank, just enjoying the moment with total peace and quiet. Although he had been to some beautiful and exotic countries, there was no place quite like home.

Just before the sun started to set, Stuart started making his way back down the hill. He felt at peace with himself. He had no feelings of guilt or regret about the things that he had done in the past. Had he been wrong to take the lives of fellow-men? No, thought Stuart, for these men killed and they ruined the lives of thousands of innocent people every year. Despite that, Stuart knew that to play the role of the judge, the jury and the executioner, was no longer for him. He would leave that to the Russell Hodges of the world.

11

When Stuart returned to the hotel he found D.S Jones at the reception, booking himself in.

Sharon was no longer there, her shift must have finished.   Sharon had been replaced by the ever-so-polite Karen the waitress from the restaurant. Being short she could barely see over the top of the counter.

"Hello Mr Brodie. I will be with you in a moment." she said, with her ever-pleasing smile.

"Hello Stuart, how are you?" said Jones
"Fine thanks" replied Stuart not wanting to start a conversation. D.S. Jones must have picked up on this, for once he got the key to his room he quickly left. After Jones left the foyer, Stuart realised that D.C. Black was not with him. He was quite glad for he did not like that man. He had attitude, a smart-arse, and the type that would bully people smaller than himself. It was policemen like Black that gave the public a bad impression and the lack of trust in the police.

When Stuart arrived at the dining room, Ryan was waiting. Stuart's curt response earlier had obviously not deterred Jones.

"Hello Stuart, mind if I eat with you and we can talk?"

"OK" replied Stuart feeling cornered.

During dinner Stuart and Ryan spoke very little. But, afterwards over a few drinks, Stuart started to relax and chat about Asia. Ryan putting him at his ease, then Ryan manoeuvred the conversation around to the men killed in London. Before Stuart would talk he wanted an assurance that the talk was in confidence. He told Ryan that he would never go on record and never testify. Ryan gave him that assurance

Stuart admitted that he knew all of the men through Rick Maynard; he had either met them in London when he collected money for Rick or out in Asia when Rick introduced them as business associates.

Ryan questioned Stuart about the money, and Stuart told Ryan that he had thought he was just doing Rick a favour but of course he now realised that the money was to fund Rick's drug operation.

"But, you knew it was a drug ring and didn't report it?" Ryan accused Stuart.

Stuart defended himself "I was going to but Rick was killed and the ring collapsed, they were not going to be dealing drugs again and I didn't want to get involved and find myself back in jail"

"Maybe so Stuart but it would have been good to get some of the other members"

"You would have been too late, I think Russell got to them first" said Stuart smiling.

A commotion and the bar interrupted their conversation. Mike Guilds, an alcoholic, had fallen off a bar stool, which he did periodically. No-one ever realised how drunk he was until he fell. It was sad to see a young person in such a state, for he was only in his early twenties. Apparently he had been in the army, where he had witnessed some tragic events. He had turned to drink, which now sadly ruled his life. The locals had a saying they used when describing how drunk someone was, they referred to them as being Micky Guild.

Once the bar had settled down

Stuart asked Jones "How were the murder victims killed?"

"I can't tell you that Stuart, you must realise" replied Jones.

"OK, well just nod if I am correct then." Stuart quickly described a couple of Russell's known execution methods.

Ryan inclined his head slightly.

Even if there had been little doubt before, now Stuart was in no doubt the killer was Russell Hodges.

The method of execution Russell used depended upon the location of the hit.

In the jungle he would always use a gun and finish them off by shooting in the head. Shooting people in London however could be a bit risky, it could draw unnecessary attention.

Russell would opt for the silent method. Two of the victims had had their necks broken, caused by a fatal blow. Stuart knew that all Russell needed was his hands. He had witnessed this on several occasions, Russell delivering such a blow with his hand to the side of the neck, with such speed and force, the victim was dead before they hit the ground; as quick as a blink of the eye.

The other two victims had their spinal cords severed by inserting a small blade between the last vertebrae and skull. This was a technique that Stuart used himself when dispatching a wounded deer. It was quick, painless and caused very little bleeding. Yes, thought Stuart, these were the trademarks of a very dangerous man and Jones was going to need all the help he could get, if he was going catch him. Not much chance of catching Russell though, thought Stuart. Russell Hodges was ex army turned hit-man and he was as professional as they come.

12

Ryan said good-night to Stuart and returned to his room. He had plenty to think about. Stuart had confirmed the identity of the hit-man, or had he? How did Stuart know the execution method? Maybe the hit-man was Stuart? "Now, I'm getting paranoid" thought Ryan "I'll sleep on it hopefully I will be thinking clearly in the morning".

The first night that Ryan had stayed at the Braes of Brackie Hotel, he had not slept well. For in the room there had been an over-powering smell of lavender, which came from bunches of the stuff that hung in the wardrobes. Or maybe it had been the presence of Chris Black that had kept him awake, or both? Ryan did not care for the man, he was too abrupt and always in a rush, desperate for promotion. Ryan had sent him back to London and tonight he would get rid of the lavender.

Despite the absence of both the Lavender and Chris Black, Ryan found sleep would not come, instead he found his mind drifting back to his first case with the C.I.D that too had been a drug- related, gangland murder a case that took almost a year to solve.

Ryan would always remember the first day at C.I.D. It started at eight thirty in the morning, at the North London police head-quarters. The introductions had been brief, as word came in that a body had been discovered in the back of a van. It turned out that the van had actually been stolen. When the thief discovered what was in the back of the van, he abandoned it and notified the police. Ryan had been given the task of tracking down the thief, which he achieved successfully the same day. The body in the back of the van had been a shocking sight. Not only had he been shot several times, but his head had been split wide open. The blow with the machete had been delivered with such force, that it had split the head from the top of the skull right down into the neck. The machete had been left lodged in the young man's body. Not a pretty sight for anyone to find.

Ryan realised that the thief who stole the van would have been totally shocked when he saw what was in the back of it. The vomit on the passenger's seat confirmed this.

Ryan also guessed that whoever made the gruesome discovery would find it hard to keep quiet about it. The thief, apart from wanting to tell someone about his ordeal, would more likely than not want a few strong drinks.

So Ryan started with his enquiries at the local bars. By mid-afternoon, Ryan found the van-thief in a rather drunken state, so drunk that Ryan had to wait until the next day before the thief could be questioned and subsequently charged.

It was a quick result for Ryan but the murderer killed another three men in the very same way, before being finally apprehended. The machete was his trade mark and it was also to be his downfall.

Not only were the machetes handmade, they were made from a certain type of stainless steel, the type of steel that was used for making industrial ovens D.C. Ryan Jones had the task of visiting the five Factories that made industrial ovens, three of which were in the Midlands and the other two in the north of England. It turned out that the steel came from one of the Factories in the Midlands.

With the source of the steel confirmed, Ryan set about checking the history of all the staff that worked there. In total there were seventeen full-time workers and six part-time. The fulltime workers were all long-serving employees. Their time at the Factory ranged from nine to twenty six years. The part-time workers consisted of two men who were semi-retired and the other four were students. The part-time staff worked four nights a week. Their job was mainly keeping the Factory clean. The two semi-retired men did however on occasion, cut and shape steel to specific sizes.

After weeks of intensive interviewing at the Factory, Ryan finally got a lead. One of the semi-retired workers admitted to having cut steel once or twice for a workmate, but it wasn't for use in making ovens. His workmate's hobby was knife-making and when Ryan questioned the workmate about his hobby, the workmate admitted to having made the machetes. The person that he made the machetes for was a farmer that ran a very large vegetable farm.

The farmer had ordered and paid for three dozen of the specially-made machetes, but when Ryan had questioned the farmer, he found that only thirty of the machetes were accounted for. The person that had access and used the machetes no longer worked at the farm. The farmer had told Ryan that he could see no reason why Jubo would steal the machetes. He also told Ryan that he had been disappointed when Jubo left as Jubo had been a very useful worker, but sadly he had to return to Jamaica to sort out some family business. This of course had been a lie. Instead of going to Jamaica he had gone to London and it wasn't to top and tail turnips, with his nice new shiny machetes.

Ryan eventually caught up with and arrested Jubo. Six months later Jubo was battered to death in prison. It was obviously a revenge killing from the drug underworld.

When Ryan had heard about the death of Jubo, it came as no great surprise to him and he felt no pity for him whatsoever. During interrogation, Jubo had taken great pleasure in telling Ryan exactly how he carried out the murders.

He would shoot his victims several times in the lower part of the body with a 9mm hand gun, which was powerful enough to cause serious injury. With his victim seriously injured and disabled, he would then read them the last rights, his own version. Jubo told Ryan that when they heard his version of the last rights, they would cry and beg him for mercy and do anything to try and stay alive. He told them to get up onto their knees, put their arms by their sides, look up to heaven and pray. It was at that point that Jubo would bring the machete crashing down through their skulls. He was to be the most brutal and sadistic killer that Ryan Jones ever encountered.

13

Probably unwisely and after one too many glasses of Merlot, Stuart had agreed to let Jones go stalking with him in the morning.

Back in the jungles of Asia, Russell had shown good stalking skills. He was totally switched on. He would take in every detail of his surroundings, reading the signs, always alert. Russell could move through the thickest of cover with such ease, never making a sound and with such speed and grace. When the time came, he would not hesitate in making his kill. Yes, thought Stuart, Russell would make one hell of a good deer stalker. I wonder how Jones will do.

"Morning." said Stuart as Jones arrived in the deserted hall.

"Good morning. What about breakfast?"

"No time. The chef made up sandwiches for us. Before we head off I just want to point out a few things okay. First of all, if you have your mobile phone with you, switch it off now. Second no talking unless I do. If you have anything in your pockets that might jingle, like keys or coins, leave them here and stay behind me at all times unless I say otherwise okay? Now have you fired a full bore rifle before?"

"No, only a .22 on rabbits and that was a long time ago. I am not bothered about shooting a deer. I just want to see how it is done."

"That's fine by me. Now have you any questions?"

"No." "Okay then, let's go." It was still dark out-side, the weather was dry and mild, with a slight breeze coming in from the sea. The conditions were good for stalking.

Leaving the land rover, Stuart slowly made his way to the edge of the wood, ensuring that he didn't stand on any dead branches or twigs. Ryan did the same, keeping about three paces behind Stuart. At the edge of the wood, Stuart crouched down low, behind a large Scots Pine tree. Looking behind him, Stuart noticed that Ryan had also crouched down, about five feet behind. Peering round the side of the tree, Stuart scanned first the edge of the wood, then the hillside.

There were a number of deer visible on the hillside. The closest deer were around two hundred yards away and about fifty yards from the trees. Stuart decided he would go for these the nearest first. Quietly, Stuart slipped the bolt up and down then slowly raised himself upright. After putting in his ear plugs, Stuart slid round the tree. Using the large Scots Pine as a rest, Stuart brought the rifle to his shoulder and took aim. The crack from the .270 echoed along the hillside, confusing the deer as to what direction they should run. Stuart shot four of the stags before they could make their escape into the wood.

"So what do you think so far Ryan?"

"I am suitably impressed and also glad I am not a deer"

"If you were, you wouldn't know what hit you" said Stuart with a smile.

"No I don't suppose, I would" said Ryan giving a slight shiver at the thought.

They ventured out onto the hill. Stuart had told Ryan there might be a chance of a few stragglers still out although after hearing the shots, any deer that were close-by would have scampered back into the wood. After walking for almost an hour, they came upon a lone stag still grazing.

Stuart asked Ryan if he would like a shot. He said that he would and Stuart explained the procedure to him.

"Wait until the stag is broadside on, place the cross-hairs behind the line of the front leg about four inches up the rib cage, then slip the safety-catch off, hold the rifle firmly into your shoulder, hold your breath and squeeze the trigger."

"Okay." said Ryan slowly nodding his head. A few minutes passed then boom went the rifle and down went the beast. Ryan let out his breath, which seemed more like a sigh of relief. This was the first time he had shot anything larger than a rabbit.

"You shot it, now you can gralloch It." said Stuart with a grin on his face. Ryan looked puzzled

"Gut it" said Stuart laughing

Ryan had watched Stuart closely when he 'gralloched' the beasts earlier, so he set about the task. When he had finished, Stuart told him that he had done a good job.

"But look here, you missed a bit." said Stuart crouching over the dead animal, encouraging Ryan to do the same. Then as quick as a flash Stuart scooped a handful of blood from inside the carcass and smeared both Ryan's cheeks with the blood. Ryan jumped back.

"What the fuck are you doing?" said Ryan in a very angry tone.

"Don't panic, it's a tradition when someone shoots their first deer, you know, first blood and all that." said Stuart who was having a bit of a laugh.

Ryan joined in, although he was not over-keen at laughing at himself. Ryan knew that Stuart was doing his job, but he couldn't help notice that Stuart seemed to have certain ruthlessness about him. Or maybe it was just professionalism. Either way, Ryan realised Stuart was just as much a killer as Russell Hodges and he wondered just how many people Stuart had killed back in Asia, for he was sure he was a killer.

Still, maybe there was a bit of killer in us all, thought Ryan, after all hadn't he had just killed an innocent animal.

Back at the Land Rover, Stuart called Steve to tell him where the five stags lay and Ryan checked his mobile for messages.

"Shit!"

"What's wrong?"

"There's been another murder, only this time it's in Glasgow and it seems to have the same hallmarks as the others. It looks like your friend has moved north of the border Stuart.

Silence fell as they got into the Land Rover and hardly a word was spoken as they drove back to the hotel. They were both deep in thought. The executioner had arrived.

14

Ryan made some calls and rapidly gathered details of the latest victim. His name was Gerald Bowman and he was a prominent Glaswegian businessman. The man owned several properties and various businesses on the west coast. He must somehow be connected to the other murder victims as he had been killed in the same way as two of them, with a fatal blow to the side of the neck. But, this man was not known as having any connection to drugs or organized crime. In police parlance he was 'clean'. This murder did not fit the pattern. He decided that he would head through to Glasgow and get more details on the case.

Stuart stood chatting to Ryan as Ryan checked out of the hotel. Sharon was back on duty and Stuart noticed she was not her usual cheerful self. Assuming he was the cause, he felt a bit guilty about the off-hand way he treated her the day before.

Stuart attempted to get her attention, thinking I am probably going to regret this,

"Is everything okay Sharon? You don't seem your normal self today?"

"Yes I am fine; it's just what I heard on the radio at lunch time, about the murder of Gerald Bowman in Glasgow."

"Why? Did you know the man?" asked Ryan taking a sudden interest.

"Yes he used to stay here sometimes. He used to meet with Peter Grant the Factor and two other people. I don't know much about the others as they never stayed here." said Sharon, a little uncomfortable with the questioning. Ryan noted this but carried on.

"Have you any idea what their meetings were about Sharon?"

"Not really, I imagine that it was to do with some business or other."

"Any idea what sort of business?"

Sharon shrugged "All I know is that the bill was made out to Caledonian Land Holdings, which the Factor always took with him. He said that he would hand it in as the company rented an office at his farm."

"Okay, thanks a lot Sharon." said Ryan not wanting to push too hard, but he could tell she was holding back.

Stuart, who had been listening in, also realised Sharon was holding back and determined to use their relationship to find out more. Ryan was thinking along similar lines. He badly needed to make headway in this case.

Outside in the foyer, Ryan turned to Stuart. "I've to go to Glasgow, but I should be back either tonight or tomorrow. Maybe I shouldn't ask you this, but I know you get on well with Sharon. I was wondering if you could speak to her, see if you can find out anything more, especially about the other two men. Their names must have been mentioned at some point. They may even be in danger, if Russell Hodges is after them and gets to them before we do"

Then Ryan had another thought "How well do you know the Factor?" he asked.

"I suppose I know him pretty well, but only through work I don't know him socially. I must admit I wasn't aware that he came here every month for meetings"

"You would have thought that you would have bumped into them by now though, at least once or twice"

"I was just thinking that myself"

"When you come over to this part of the estate Stuart, does the Factor tell you which days to come?"

"Yes that's right"

"So he knows where you are at all times, though I suppose most bosses like to know where their staff are, probably not important. Anyway, would you speak to Sharon find out what she knows?"

"Okay I will see what I can do." said Stuart.

"And by the way Stuart thanks for taking me out stalking today. It was very educational. I enjoyed it very much.

"Anytime." said Stuart as they parted company.

Stuart returned to the reception "Sharon would you like to meet later for a drink and a chat?"

"I don't know Stuart, it's a bit awkward with the children, we'll see."

"Okay, you know where to find me if you do."

As Ryan left for Glasgow he was thinking hard. Is Stuart Brodie involved with Russell Hodges? Is the Factor simply an innocent bystander caught up in this? Who are Caledonian Land Holdings? Well first things first he would find out all he could about that company.

Stuart went to the gun room where he gave his rifle a clean and locked it away. What was Sharon's involvement in all this? She seems very concerned about the death of the chap from Glasgow. Perhaps she had something going with him.

Stuart was now keen to speak to her and get some answers. But, she didn't seem very enthusiastic when he'd asked her for a drink, unlike the last time.

"Up to her" thought Stuart.

15

Stuart spent that evening in the bar, waiting for Sharon who never showed. Frustrated, he went to his room. Oh well he thought he might have to sweet talk her a bit tomorrow in order to get back into her good books and get the information from her. Stuart was determined.

As Stuart drifted into sleep, he thought he heard a tap on the door. Looking at the clock he saw that it was just past midnight. The gentle tapping continued, with a sigh Stuart got up and put on his robe. Answering the door he found a very distressed Sharon.

Stuart put his arms around her and pulled her into his room.

"What's the matter" he asked with concern.

"The Factor called to tell me Gerald Bowman was dead.

"Why would the Factor call you?" Stuart asked.

"The Factor and Gerald were friends, like I told D.S Jones earlier. They used to meet here along with two others every month"

"Who were the other two men?"

"It was a man and a woman, I only knew them as Catherine and Martin. They seemed pleasant enough."

"So why are you so upset Sharon? Is there something else that you want to talk about?"

Sharon was now crying into her cupped hands and shaking. "I feel that I have just made such a fool of myself, and now I feel like I am just about to lose everything, my house and the kids" "What do you mean?" enquired Stuart genuinely puzzled.

"Well after John my husband died, I was feeling really down and needed a shoulder to cry on. Peter who had always been nice to us he had even given us one of his cottages to live in practically rent-free. Anyway, he came round to see me and told me not to worry about the rent, for all it was anyway. He said I could stay there for as long as I wanted and like I said, I needed a shoulder to cry on. Peter was there and one thing led to the other. I knew he was married but I didn't care. I just wanted someone to hold and comfort me. So we started having an affair. After a while, I realised that I would never be anything more to him than a mistress. He never took me out and he barely spoke to me at the hotel. He only came to me when he wanted sex. So I broke it off last year and now he phones to tell me about Gerald and says that if I want to keep my cottage, I had better keep my mouth shut and not mention that we had an affair or anything about Gerald and the others. I feel scared Stuart. I don't know what to do."

"Well I think that you should speak to D.S. Jones. Tell him what you just told me. Maybe he can help, especially if the Factor is threatening you. Maybe go and stay with your sister for a while; at least until you find another place to live, because I think the sooner you are out of the Factor's grip the better. Meanwhile try not to worry" said Stuart thinking to himself that he could do without this, for he had enough problems of his own.

"O God, I wish John was still alive. We were so happy together and none of this would have happened."

"Your husband died in a fishing accident didn't he?"

"Yes, fishing was his life. He loved the sea and the children. Mind you, he was not his usual self before he died.

"Why not?" asked Stuart.

"I am not sure, but he became very moody. Maybe he was just bored. He said that catching fish had become more like a pastime than a business."

"How do you mean Sharon?"

"Well, he said that they spent most of their time delivering animal feeds or picking them up. I went to meet John at the harbour one time, he seemed so miserable. They were unloading the boat and putting the bags onto the Factor's lorry. He breeds rare sheep or something. He has one of those Lorries where the back folds down like a small cattle float"

"Did the Factor own the fishing boat?" enquired Stuart, curious now.

"No all the boats belong or rather belonged to Gerald Bowman. He had three fishing boats and a ferry that goes back and forward to Ireland. John and I took the kids over once"

Sharon started crying again, obviously brought on by the memories of happier times.

"What else did the Factor say?" asked Stuart putting his arm around her.

"The Factor asked if the police were here and told me not to say anything to them about Gerald and the others and for some reason, never to mention Caledonian Land Holdings. Oh what is going on Stuart?" said Sharon pressing herself even tighter against him.

"Promise me that you will speak with D.S Jones tomorrow" was all Stuart could say in comfort. Besides he was now starting to get aroused with the closeness of Sharon's body.

Sharon promised through her tears that she would speak to Jones. She felt safe in Stuart's arms sensing his desire, and the feeling was mutual, giving into their desire they made love into the small hours of the morning.

Stuart's last thoughts before sleep were that even if Sharon didn't he would speak to Ryan and pass on the new-found information. Stuart had a slight feeling of guilt about, perhaps taking advantage of Sharon in her vulnerable state and how he had come by the new information. But, Sharon had come to him. She had been only too willing to confide in him, easing the heavy load that she seemed to be carrying on her shoulders. He could deal with Ryan for her.

Sharon, as she had done on their previous encounter, slipped away in the darkness of the night. Stuart was awake this time, but didn't let on. He felt it better to pretend that he was sleeping.

This way it would save any embarrassment, for he knew that Sharon still had some pride left. She would certainly not like to be thought of as some cheap tart who visits men in their bedrooms in the middle of the night. So Stuart let her slip out of room.

Before she left, Sharon leant over the bed and gave Stuart a gentle kiss on the cheek. She whispered something in his ear, but Stuart couldn't make it out. The door closed with a gentle click, Sharon was gone.

Within minutes Stuart fell into a deep sleep.

16

Stuart called Ryan Jones in the morning the second Ryan answered the call Stuart asked "How did you get on digging up dirt on Caledonian Land Holdings"

Ryan admitted he had not been able to find out anything about the company. Ryan surmised that it must be a private company as it was not registered at Company's House. He had set one of his team in London the task of digging up anything they could.

Ryan was interested to know if Stuart had got any information from Sharon. Stuart quickly filled him in on his conversation with Sharon, including the fact that the Factor has threatened Sharon and warned her never to mention Caledonian Land Holdings or Gerald Bowman.

"That's great Stuart, well done. Look, there isn't much I can do here in Glasgow. The local C.I.D. said they will follow their own line of inquiries. They don't need me, or more to the point they don't want me around. So what I think I will do is pay your Factor a visit. I take it you will be going stalking today?"

"Yes but I will be back in time for dinner" replied Stuart.

"By the way Stuart, Sharon mentioned the Factor has a farm and that Bowman's company rents an office at the farm. What can you tell me about the farm?"

"Well, it belongs to the Factor he has had it for about ten years. I have never been to it as it is not part of the estate. The Factor has a sideline business, he breeds rare sheep" Stuart explained. "And this farm is where the sheep business is based?"

"Where is this farm Stuart?" asked Ryan

"It is about 20 miles north west of Brackie Woods. It is called Bonnie Doone Farm"

"Thanks, I'll catch you up later. Have a good day Stuart."

"And you, bye."

Stuart switched off his mobile he liked Ryan, which was strange, for with his past he never would have believed he could befriend a policeman.

He thought he would give Sharon a call, he knew he was getting involved there too but he couldn't just use her and completely abandon her. The phone rang over to voicemail. Stuart left a brief message telling Sharon he had spoken to Jones and things would be Ok. A reassurance he didn't entirely believe.

Sharon heard the phone but ignored it, she continued to stare blankly into the bathroom mirror the reflection showed a very distressed, tear-stained face, her face was huge, puffed up from several hours of continuous crying. Her blue eyes were red-rimmed. "What a mess" thought Sharon, as she swept the strands of her matted blonde hair from her face.

"What am I going to do?" asked Sharon of her reflection.

"Just look at you. What a bloody mess you're in" the reflection seemed to answer back. "It's time you got a grip of yourself girl. After all you have still got the kids. Forget about men, for they are all bastards, even Stuart Brodie. All they want is one thing; an easy shag. Well no more. Here's what you do girl; have a shower, smarten yourself up and then go and join the kids at your sister's, okay?"

"Right that's exactly what I am going to do." Sharon managed a weak smile. "My God, I am talking to myself in the mirror they'll lock me up"

Sharon turned from the mirror and headed towards the bedroom with a more positive attitude.

17

Ryan Jones arrived at the Factor's office just before midday. He had called first thing that morning to arrange a time that best suited the Factor.

He was greeted by Christine who was expecting him. As she quickly ushered him along to the Factor's office, she informed him that the Factor was very busy today, letting Ryan know that this was going to be a brief meeting.

The Factor told Ryan that he had rented an office to Gerald Bowman, for a short time, years ago and that he had not seen or heard from Bowman since. Ryan armed with the latest information from Sharon knew that was a lie, The Factor denied any knowledge of the other murder victims. Ryan decided to spook the Factor; he unexpectedly asked "So what about Caledonian Land Holdings? I understand you have a business connection with them"

"No I am sorry I don't know what you are talking about – no idea" replied the Factor smooth but not quite able to disguise the fleeting look of shock.

"Now if you don't mind I must get on, Christine will show you out" the Factor was dismissive and keen for Ryan to be gone.

"Now if you don't mind I must get on, Christine will show you out" the Factor was keen for Jones to be gone.

Jones decided to go, he didn't want to press too hard, not yet. He wanted to speak with Stuart and find out more about his chat with Sharon and then speak to her. However,

Ryan interest had been piqued by the information from Stuart about the Factor's farm and now after this unsatisFactory interview he was even more interested in the Factor and all his business dealings. The Factor was hiding something whether it was illegal or just unethical, Ryan wasn't sure. He had no evidence to connect the Factor with drug running or the killings in London. But, Ryan knew the Factor was up to something and he would dig deeper until he found out what it was. Ryan decided he would go by the farm for a snoop on his way back to the hotel.

As soon as Ryan left the Factor made a phone call to police Superintendent Blake of Glasgow Police. Blake was an old acquaintance of the Factor, she and the Factor's sister had gone to the same private school.

The Factor told her to call Ryan off, "Tell the London cops to keep out of Scottish affairs. Get D.S. Jones back to London where he belongs. I do not want to see him on my estate again, understood" the Factor raged down the phone.

"Yes Peter", Blake tried to calm him down "I will call his boss in London and telling him Jones is being unconstructive in our investigations and we don't need him. I will insist on his immediate recall."

"Okay, well do it. I have enough problems to deal with at the moment"

The Factor slammed down the phone, thought for a moment, grimaced then made another call "I have a problem I need you to take care off" he said.

18

It took Ryan quite some time to find the Bonnie Doone farm, it was not signposted, he asked at a roadside cottage and at a village shop but no one seemed to have heard of it. As a last resort he tried a side-road marked as a 'Private Road'. The road went on for at least five miles winding its way through a glen to the back of beyond. At the end of the road, Ryan was met by a large gate. On the gate was a large rectangular sign and written in bold letters were the words 'PRIVATE. KEEP OUT' on either side of the gate ran an eight or nine foot chain-link fence with barbed wire on the top and the ominous posted warning "danger electrified fence". Ryan reckoned this must be the place. He could see the farm buildings in the distance, there was a reasonable-sized stone-built house, and several out-buildings, to the sides of the farm buildings, there were five or six paddocks. In these sheep of various sizes and colours grazed peacefully.

Ryan got out of his car an approached the gate, he noticed CCTV cameras and an intercom system. Ryan thought the security seemed a bit over the top for sheep. It was the type of security usually reserved for military operations.

Suddenly the intercom crackled.

"Can I help you" said the disembodied voice, stern and unfriendly. Ryan was momentarily caught off guard. "Ah yes, I was wondering if you can help me. I am looking for a Mr Chris Black." the first name that came into Ryan's head.

"Sorry, there is no one by that name who works here I have ever heard of him. Try the local shop or something." The intercom went dead. Ryan had seen enough anyway, to guess that this was the Factor's farm.

Not an easy place to enter undetected, thought Ryan. There were no trees, or any other type of cover within a half mile radius of the farm. The nearest hills were about a mile away. But then again, with powerful binoculars it could be possible to get a clear view of the farm from those hills.

Ryan turned his car and headed back through the glen thinking about the farm's location he realised that there was only one way in or out of the farm. So if he should manage to get a search warrant he should be able to ensure that no-one escaped out the 'back way'. "But is that confidence, or stupidity" Ryan said aloud to himself as he reached the end of the single-track road. But Ryan had missed something, something that was tucked behind the farm buildings out of sight.

When Ryan arrived back at the hotel, he was shocked to hear news of a tragic accident earlier that day. He also received a rather irate phone call from his boss in London.

19

That evening when Stuart returned to the hotel, Ryan was waiting for him. Ryan looked grim.

"Stuart I have some news for you, it's not good, perhaps you would like a whisky"

Ryan motioned to Karen to get Stuart a whisky. Stuart noticed Karen's eyes were red.

"What's going on?" he thought with the first stirrings of alarm "My kids..."

"It's Sharon Stuart, she was in an accident. They took her to hospital, they did everything they could but she died on the operating table"

It didn't register at first.

"But...I was with her last night" Stuart shook his head

"Poor Sharon" thought Stuart "All she wanted out of life was a bit of love and affection and a good home to bring up her kids. She'd had her share of tragedy when her husband died. Maybe she had been out to get whatever she could from men, and looked to them to solve her problems, but so what? That is common enough in woman"

"What happened?" asked Stuart still stunned.

"The car left the road and crashed down an embankment, maybe it was run off the road Forensics is there now. A blue 4x4 was seen in the vicinity" Ryan filled in the details

"Her children?" asked Stuart.

"They were with her sister, still are, the sister is going to take care of them now Stuart absently drank the whisky lost in thought. 'It's a very unpredictable and unjust world in which we live, he knew that only too well, having crossed the line a few times. He knew when to quit, but even after quitting, he was living with the knowledge of his past and has to cope with his conscience. Not an easy task for some. Maybe Sharon couldn't cope? Maybe she had crashed the car herself?"

Ryan interrupted Stuart's thoughts "Do you think it could have been Russell Hodges, could it be linked to the case?"

"No way" dismissed Stuart "Russell would make sure she was dead. He wouldn't let her die in hospital, he wouldn't take that chance'

Ryan nodded accepting the reasoning.

"Let's go through to the bar, somewhere more private" said Ryan.

Once settled at their usual table in front of the fire, Ryan filled Stuart in on what had happened at the Factor's.

"I had a chat with your Factor this morning, but to no avail, he denied any knowledge of Bowman, other than he had once rented him an office, which we already knew. He also denied any knowledge of Caledonian Land Holdings. On the way back, I went to his farm which is not far from here. The place is like Fort Knox. I could not even get past the front gate. I am going to see if I can get a search warrant, although that might be a bit difficult."

"Why?" said Stuart with a puzzled frown.

"I have been summoned back to London, what for, I don't know. My boss was very evasive, not like him at all; in fact he seemed a bit pissed-off. I don't know when I will be back, if at all. My advice to you Stuart, not that you need any, is watch your back. If they killed Sharon in fear that she might have told me what she knew then who knows,

even you could be in danger. I will keep in touch" said
Ryan

Ryan felt disappointed, he hated to be leaving the
case, leaving Scotland and Stuart. Was Stuart in danger?
Ryan was concerned, although he still hadn't ruled Stuart
out as complicit in the drugs or the murders or both. After
all he was probably the last man to see Sharon alive, so must
be considered a suspect, if it turned out to be foul play.
Ryan couldn't help but like Stuart even though he knew
Stuart was no angel.

20

The next day Stuart went out stalking in Brackie Wood, known locally as the big wood, it was an eerie place and today, it seemed even more so with a dense mist swirling and obscuring the paths and the trees.

It was a difficult area for deer stalking.

The wood had been planted on the side of the hill, taking in some thirty acres consisting mainly of mature Scots Pine and Norway Spruce, with Birch trees growing along the side of paths and in any open spaces.

Throughout the wood were rocky areas, with small natural caves created from large boulders that had came to rest during the thaw from the ice age all those years ago, the caves had provided over the centuries homes for bears and wolves and whatever else roamed the land.

The wood was never bright always at least in semi darkness. In the low lying areas were wet mud-holes which the deer used these as wallow holes to cool down in the summer and rid themselves of ticks. Around the mud-holes lingered the strong musky odour of the stags.

It never failed to amaze Stuart was how easily and quietly the large stags could negotiate their way through the wood. All Stuart would catch is a fleeting glimpse, a blur or their shadow. They were the ghosts in the wood.

Suddenly Stuart sensed he wasn't alone he froze and felt the hairs on the back of his neck rise. He turned imperceptibly, slowly, and at the edge of his vision he saw what appeared to be a figure which slipped in behind a large tree, about ten yards from where he stood. Stuart moved off the track into the wood, on the same side as the mystery figure, he felt safer within the trees. Crouching on one knee he looked and listened for any sign of movement.

The adrenalin was beginning to rush through his veins, just as it had done in the jungle, not sure of what to expect next. A cold sweat began to form on his brow. Someone was watching him. Was it Russell? The figure had disappeared without making a sound or leaving any clue as to where it had gone.

Should he follow, track it down and risk walking into an ambush? No, thought Stuart. If it was Russell, he would confront Stuart when he was ready. Stuart the deer stalker was now being stalked. This sent a shiver down Stuart's spine, was he the prey and Russell the predator?

Stuart headed for one of the four high seats that he and Steve had strategically positioned throughout the wood. The seats were for a single person, they were eight feet tall, constructed from tubular steel and painted green to help blend in with the landscape.

The high seat was situated in a large clearing, known as a deer lawn, an area into which deer would come to graze. This clearing had been created after a violent storm, many years ago. Sometimes the lawns were deliberately created in order to entice the deer to these areas where they could be easily shot.

Stuart was uncomfortable with the idea that Russell was prowling about in the wood and didn't relish the thought of bumping into him. So, Stuart reasoned that sitting up in the high seat would give him the advantage, for Stuart knew that Russell wouldn't want to break cover, an additional bonus for Stuart was with Russell on the prowl a deer or two might be flushed into the clearing.

"Things are bad" thought Stuart "I am being watched and the watcher is a professional killer. I have a sinking feeling that I might be on death row"

Despite his situation Stuart was calm almost fatalistic. Back In the jungles of Asia, he had accepted the possibility of death and knew it might be swift and unexpected. He also knew that he was no match for Russell if Russell wanted him dead he would die. But he was still alive and that comforted Stuart. When Russell was on a job, Russell was not one to play games. The fact that Stuart wasn't already dead was a good sign, a small hope for Stuart to cling to.

.

21

While Stuart was in the woods Ryan set off to catch his flight to Heathrow. He had driven only a few miles from the Braes of Brackie Hotel when he noticed a parked car near the spot of Sharon's accident.

Ryan slowed down and saw a young woman at the roadside, sitting with her knees pulled tightly into her chest her chin resting on her knees. In the back of the car, Ryan could see the slightly bowed heads of two young children, all were sitting motionless.

An overwhelming sadness gripped Ryan, and he knew that the children were Sharon's and the young woman crouching by the roadside was her sister. Ryan knew how they felt the pain of his wife's death cut through him again. He wanted to stop but knew his words of comfort would be inadequate. He drove on leaving them alone to mourn in peace.

Reaching the airport he bought a local paper to read on the flight. He looked for an article on the Bowman murder but nothing. "This is being kept very quiet" he thought "It's unusual to be able to keep the press completely off the trail". He wondered who was pulling strings and why.

The flight was on time and arrived at Heathrow in good time. The weather in London was cold and foggy with a light drizzle of rain. D.C Chris Black was there to meet him.

"I bet you're glad to be back to civilisation." said Chris in his usual arrogant way. Ryan just agreed with him as he could not be bothered speaking to him, his thoughts were elsewhere, back in Scotland, for he was missing the place already, especially the case. He felt frustrated if only he had a free reign to investigate he would get to the bottom of what was going on

"So we can let the bloody sheep shaggers get on with it. With a bit of luck, they will all fucking kill each other" sneered Chris.

"You know Chris you are such a twat at times, you'll be lucky to see any promotion with your attitude."

"Well, they are a bunch of heathens and you have to admit, they are a bit behind the times" Chris defended himself.

"I disagree with you completely. You obviously don't know much about history do you? Some of the greatest inventors in the world are Scottish. Now just shut the fuck up and drive."

Much to Ryan's delight, Chris didn't say another word for the remainder of the journey. He was obviously in a huff. Chris drove Ryan to his two bedroom garden flat in Camden, North London. Ryan thanked Chris for the ride realising he might have been a bit hard on him but try as he might Ryan couldn't take to Chris at all.

Steps led from the street down to the flat's small front garden. June has loved the garden and when she was alive it was a riot of colour all year round, even in winter June would have plant tubs of evergreens with their winter berries.

Ryan opened the door to the flat. The flat was quite large in addition to the garden at the front there was a small kitchen garden at the rear. It had two large bedrooms in addition to a small room Ryan used as his office, it house an old computer system, printer and telephone.

The flat was comfortably furnished but had a neglected air. The floors were striped oak through out. In the living room were two comfortable leather sofas on top of a bright rug, bookcases lined one wall, June had been an avid reader. A television stood in one corner and on a cherry sideboard sat a state of the art stereo system. Both Ryan and June had loved blues and jazz, Ryan hardly listened to music now too many memories. An antique fireplace housed a realistic gas fire. Ryan turned it on but to him the room was always cold and cheerless without June.

Ryan made himself coffee in the sparse kitchen, when June was here the counter tops were filled with spices, oils, breads and fruit. Now it housed a jar of instant coffee and Ryan lived off takeaways and microwave meals.

Ryan thought about the case in Scotland "The Factor is involved in something but maybe not murder or drugs. It could be just simple greed I wouldn't mind looking into the venison distribution business a bit more, I bet he has a scam going on there. At the very least it is a conflict of interest but I wonder if it is illegal. Still not my case anymore. Forget Scotland and get back to London life"

Ryan looked around his flat dissatisfied "I should sell this place." Ryan often thought about selling but he just couldn't let go of his family home, the place where he and June had raised their daughter, the daughter who was now settled in Canada, raising a family of her own. Ryan knew that, to keep the flat as a shrine in memory of his dead wife was wrong but he just hadn't been able to move on.

22

Ryan woke early the next morning and made his way to the police station, he knew when you were summoned to appear before Paul King, you got there sharpish or sparks would fly.

Not that Ryan was scared of King, or anyone else for that matter. He always stood his ground and fought for his corner. It was more the fact that he didn't like unnecessary confrontations.

If the truth be told, Ryan had a great deal of respect for Paul King. He knew that he was a good honest policeman. He had started at the bottom, working his way up through the ranks the hard way. This had earned him respect from the whole of the division. He knew the job inside out and his men. He didn't suffer fools gladly. They either shaped up or were shipped out.

Chief Inspector King understood the pressures of the job and the stress that it brought on. His door was always open for anyone who wanted a chat about personal problems. All in all, he wasn't a bad boss, thought Ryan.

Ryan arrived at the police station in plenty of time. It took fifteen minutes by foot and thirty by car. Ryan always chose to walk whenever he could. It helped to clear his head in the morning, plus the exercise did him good. Since being out on the hills in Scotland with Stuart, Ryan had realised that he was not as fit as he should be. He had felt the strain when he was out with Stuart, not that he had admitted that to Stuart. He had suffered in silence but he had promised himself that he would get more exercise.

At the police station Ryan was greeted with a verse from the song 'I have just came Doon frae the Isle of Sky' as he passed through the reception area. Ryan smiled at the desk sergeant and the other officers, shook his head, and made his way to Paul King's office.

Ryan was soon seated in front of his superior, Chief Inspector Paul King. Paul King was in his mid-fifties with wispy, greying hair. He stood about six feet tall and still looked in good shape for his age, albeit he had probably gained a few pounds over the years. He seemed to have small hands for his size; the hands looked as if they were permanently swollen.

This was due to the fact that he had been a boxer in his younger days, apparently a very good one at that. They say that he had great potential of becoming a world champion. Unfortunately, during one of his bouts, he knocked out his opponent and the opponent ended up in coma for three months. Paul King never fought again after that.

"What happened up in Scotland?" enquired Paul King as he scrutinized Ryan.

"It seems that I might have asked some questions to the wrong person" Ryan tried to sound apologetic.

"You certainly must have and that person is someone powerful enough to pull strings with the head of Glasgow C.I.D. She called me to say that you were interfering with her enquiry and that your presence was not welcome. I smell a rat here Ryan. Tell me what you know. You can start with Stuart Brodie. Where does he fit in?"

"Brodie worked as a money courier for Maynard, Brodie claims innocently, which explains the note I found. It was not until he met Russell Hodges that he realised it was drug money he had been transporting. Knowing there were drugs involved, he broke all ties with Maynard. Brodie told me that Hodges shot Maynard during an argument, but Brodie told me in confidence and will not go on record or repeat that in court. I am quite sure that Hodges is behind these drug related killings and Brodie is the link to Hodges" Ryan quickly re-capped.

"Now, interestingly, while I have been in Scotland, there has been one murder for certain that of Gerald Bowman and another possible murder a close friend of Brodie, Sharon Taylor. The first killing I can link to Hodges. The second according to Brodie is not Hodges's style.

We know our murders are linked to drugs and the Drug Squad have long suspect there is a drug ring operating up there. I think the whole set-up bears further investigation. In particular Brodie's boss; Peter Grant, he was involved with Bowman via a property company Caledonian Investments although he denies it. Sharon had information on their association but of course now she is dead." Ryan let the statement hang in the air.

"Do you trust Brodie?" probed Paul King.

"You know me, I trust no-one. Brodie is valuable at the moment and our only source of information on Hodges. My instinct tells me he is not involved and is scared shitless at Hodges reappearance in his life" explained Ryan with a slight grin.

"OK, good work so far Ryan."

Paul King sat silent for a moment, rubbing the knuckles on his swollen hands.

"Here's what I want you to do, I want you to return to Scotland, but keep a low profile this time okay? Try and find out as much as you can about that property company and the people involved. Meanwhile, I will speak to the boss upstairs and see what back-up can be arranged. I don't suppose you want to take D.C. Black with you again?"

Ryan shook his head. "No thanks."

"Okay, but keep me informed of what's going on and don't make a move on anything until I have got your back up sorted. If you think that you are at risk in any way, get out understand?"

"Understood"

"Okay, good luck and keep in touch"

Ryan went to his office but didn't even bother looking at the mountain of paper work on his desk. He felt excited about the case and returning to the highlands of Scotland. He felt more at home in there than he did in London.

23

Stuart's decision to sit in the high seat in the clearing paid off. Stuart had sat motionless in the high seat for almost three hours, carefully watching the clearing for any sign of movement. He was just about to call it a day, when the alarm bells began to ring.

The alarm call came from a male chaffinch at the far end of the clearing. From the chaffinch's call, Stuart could infer that a deer had possibly invaded the chaffinch's territory.

Soon Stuart spotted the cause, a large stag, the stag was street-wise, and knew how vulnerable he would be out in the open, especially in broad daylight. This wise old stag weaved his way in and out through the outer row of trees, making his way along the edge of the clearing. Stuart waited until the stag was almost at the other end of the clearing, before he shot him. From there it was but a short drag with the dead beast, to the nearest path, which was easily accessible for the Land Rover.

There had been no sign of Russell during this whole process, but Stuart suspected that Russell wasn't far away, the fact that a mature stag was active during the day, out with the rutting season, suggested that Stuart wasn't the only predator around.

Stuart was struggling to put the large stag into the back of the Land Rover when heard the clumping of heavy footsteps behind him. His nerves shattered and he froze "Can I give you a hand with that?" said a voice behind him. Stuart breathed again "Sure, I could do with a hand with this big brute. What brings you up here Steve?"

"Oh, I was getting some of that old wood for the stove back there, when I heard a shot. I figured it was you, so I took a wander up just as well seeing as how much you were struggling. Did you hear about Sharon?"

"Yes I heard."

"Bloody nice lass, so was her husband John we used to do a bit of fishing together. I didn't realise that you and Sharon had something between you until the other night"

"We were just friends. Tell me Steve, you know the Factor has a farm nearby, have you ever been to it?"

"Yes at least once a month with half a dozen deer, but I never get past the front gate. Someone always comes out and collects them. They say I can't go in because of the rare sheep. It's in case I take in some disease or other."

Steve continued "The Factor rents one of the big sheds to a meat business and they carry out the venison deliveries for him. They have three or four big vans that deliver the meat all over the place. I met one of the drivers in the pub once or twice. Come to think of it, I haven't seen him for a long time. He was a strange sort of chap anyway, from Glasgow I think. I don't know anyone else that works there. Why do you ask?"

"Just curious that's all."

Stuart suddenly felt the hairs on the back of his neck rise. He had a feeling that they were being watched. He turned round, scanning the edge of the wood. There was nothing but shadows to be seen.

"Well it will be dark soon. I better get this beast down to the larder. Jump in Steve, I can give you a lift to your truck." said Stuart, not wanting to linger in the wood any longer than need be.

More to the point, he wanted Steve out of there. Stuart didn't want Steve running into Russell.

Stuart knew that Steve could take care of himself in a scrap, he had not witnessed him in action, but he had heard the stories from the locals. Steve's reputation was that of a gentle giant, but those that knew him well said he was a gentle giant unless he was provoked and then they said he would 'lose the plot', the scrap usually ended with the locals pulling Steve off his victim before Steve could do real damage.

But, Stuart knew that if Steve ever did come up against Russell, the outcome would be inevitable. Steve wouldn't have time to lose his temper Russell would fell him like a tree.

As for his own inevitable encounter with Russell, Stuart tried not to think about it; after all, the ball was in Russell's court. Stuart stopped the Land Rover alongside Steve's pick-up truck. They both noticed at the same time. One of the back tyres was completely flat.

"Shit, look at that, I haven't had a puncture for over a year" exclaimed Steve.

"It's not the sort of place that you would expect to get a puncture. Maybe you've over-loaded the truck with wood?" asked Stuart looking for a reasonable explanation, but Stuart was worried.

"I doubt it Stuart, the wood is so dry it's like balsa wood."

They both got out of the Land Rover.

"You can carry on Stuart, I will manage this myself"

"I am sure you can Steve, but one good turn deserves another, after all you helped me with the stag."

"That's right I did, but that's just because you're getting on in years Stuart" Steve grinned at Stuart not picking up on Stuart's tension.

"Come on; let's get this fixed before it gets too dark" said Stuart ignoring Steve's gibe.

They removed the punctured tire and replaced in with a spare. Stuart was very uneasy and keen to get out of there and back to the relative safety of the Braes of Brackie. As they worked Stuart felt eyes on them, maybe his imagination was in overdrive or maybe Russell was watching, Stuart suspected the tyre had been deliberately punctured, by Russell? Was this part of a Russell's new game, a game of psychological torment?

"Tell me Steve, have you seen anyone else about in the woods?" asked Stuart

"Yes I have, actually" Steve replied.

"Who?"

"Some guy, he said that he was doing plant research in the area. I think he said that he was some kind of Doctor or other. He told me that he had permission from the estate owners."

"Are you sure that he said he had permission from the owners and not the Factor?" queried Stuart puzzled.

"I am sure that he said the owners, but I might be wrong, why? Does it really matter?"

"I like to know who is around, he could be a poacher or out to steal bird's eggs or God knows what. Not everyone is who they say they are." Stuart was spooked was this man Russell?

"Well maybe you can find out for yourself, this chap is staying at the same place you are, in fact he said that he has seen you coming and going with your rifle and he going to be careful not to get into your line of fire"

"So you told him who I was?"

"No, not really he already seemed to know, in fact he seemed to know quite a lot about the estate."

"I will have to meet the doctor whoever he is and find out what he is up to. What did he look like?"

"Hard to tell really, he was well wrapped up. I didn't get a good look at him. He was about your height maybe taller" answered Steve not very helpfully but Stuart had to be satisfied with that.

24

Stuart followed Steve's pickup truck out of the wood. His head was buzzing with new thoughts. "Shit!" thought Stuart "I forgot to ask this Doctor's name, bloody hell this situation is getting to me."

Abruptly Stuart swerved to a halt on the grass verge and reached for his mobile phone, quickly he search for a number and listened impatiently as it rang."

"Hello Peter, Stuart here."

"Hello Stuart. How are things going?"

"Things are going very well thanks. The reason I am phoning you, there is a chap over here claiming to be doing plant research. I just wanted to check that he is legit."

"What chap? Sorry Stuart I am not aware of anyone doing any research" responded the Factor a bit annoyed as he had bigger problems to deal with. "Anyway as we know only to well it is a free country now and people have the right to roam where they want we can't interfere"

"I know that Peter but I just want to make sure he isn't a poacher" explained Stuart realising that the excuse sounded very lame. "Steve met this guy who said that he has permission from the owners."

"To do what?"

"Like I said, according to Steve, he is doing a survey on plants in the area."

"This is the first that I have heard about it. Has something happened to make you suspicious of him Stuart?"

"Not really, I am just curious that's all. Steve said he seems to know quite a lot about the estate." "Maybe he knows the owners, did Steve get his name?"

"I didn't ask" Stuart realised he sounded like a fool. He told Steve he was a doctor. I take it he meant a doctor in science not in medicine. He is staying at the same hotel as I am"

"Well, there you are, if you have any concerns about this man Stuart, you can question him yourself" the Factor was eager to end the call, he wondered what was getting Stuart so worked up, maybe Sharon's death because the Factor had heard the rumours about the pair of them too.

"I will if I meet him" Stuart realised the call was going nowhere.

"Let me know if there is anything that you think I should know about" said the Factor but his tone said 'Don't bother me with trivial stuff like this again'

"I will do, bye."

Stuart drove the rest of the way to the hotel deep in thought. The doctor probably knows the owners of the estate. "Maybe it's been the doctor I have been catching sight off?" Stuart felt a moment of relief. Then he had another thought "Maybe the doctor and Russell are one and same person?" Stuart felt a tremor of fear. "But, surely Russell wouldn't take the risk of staying at the same hotel and being spotted? Then again, the doctor hasn't been spotted, well not by me anyway although he has spotted me out with my rifle. Another thing, how did he know that it was a rifle it's always in its slip except when being used? Of course he could be assuming that it's a rifle, especially if he knows a bit about the countryside. But if he has actually seen the rifle then he has probably been spying, the sneaky bugger."

Stuart parked the Land Rover in its' usual spot and inspected the cars in the hotel car park, for he was sure the doctor would have transport, the car park was quite full and included four prestigious cars two Mercedes, a Lexus and a Jaguar. Ignoring the staff cars which Stuart knew well he noted down the registration number of the rest.

On entering the hotel Stuart saw Karen at reception

"Hello Karen" Stuart greeted her as cheerfully as he could manage.

"Hello Mr Brodie, are you wanting your keys?"

"Yes, please. That's four rather prestigious cars out the back." said Stuart gesturing with his thumb in the direction of the car park.

"Yes they are very nice. They all arrived this afternoon. They are some of the people that are coming for a golden anniversary party."

"When is the party?" asked Stuart

"It's not until tomorrow night. There's going to be thirty of them altogether" Karen said rather shyly, she had a bit of a crush on Stuart but he never seemed to really notice her.

"So it will be a full house tomorrow then?"

"Yes, most of them have booked for three nights. It has come at a good time as we have been very quite lately and with Sharon's death we need to be busy to take or mind of things" Karen wanted to talk about Sharon but Stuart did not, he cut her off rather sharply.

"Will it just be me and thirty revellers over the next few days then?" probed Stuart looking for information on the doctor.

"No, there's another gentleman staying as well" replied Karen.

Stuart already knew that but he played her along "I thought that I was here all by myself."

"Not true, Dr. Russell has been here for almost a week now" Karen informed him unaware of the effect of her words.

"We have a doctor in the house do we?" said Stuart recovering well from the shock of hearing the name 'Russell' mentioned

"Not a medical doctor. He's a biologist" Karen supplied more detail.

"He sounds like an interesting person. I would like to meet him"

"Do you know this Mr Brodie; I don't think anyone has seen him since he arrived. He must come and go at strange hours."

"What about meals?"

"He doesn't eat here at all."

"Maybe he has left."

"No he sleeps in his room every night. Jane the cleaner says that his bed has always been slept in."

"He seems a rather strange fellow. I will keep an eye open for him. Anyway, I better get on. It was nice talking to you Karen."

"Have a nice evening Mr Brodie"

"I will and you, Karen."

"Good night Mr Brodie."

Stuart made his way to the gun room. The daunting thought, that Russell could be in the hotel, not only that but might have been here for a week was on his mind and sent a shiver down his spine. Tomorrow he would keep a close eye open for the elusive Dr. Russell.

25

Shortly before three the next day Ryan arrived back at Glasgow airport his flight was on time and all he had with him was hand luggage, so there was no time wasted at the baggage collection point. He picked up the hire car and headed north from the airport.

Ryan felt a sense of belonging now that he was back in Scotland. He had no idea why he felt like this. All he knew was that it felt good to be back, breathing in the nice cool fresh air and appreciating the laid-back pace of life. Once more he was away from the rat race, the stinking fumes, the suffocating feeling that plagued him every day.

Yes, it was good to be back, Ryan thought to himself. He wondered how long his stay would be for this time. He was hoping that it would be a bit longer than the last trip. Not that he wanted the case to drag on, as far as that was concerned the sooner the case was cleared the better. He might take a few days leave at the end of it that would be good. Perhaps Stuart would invite him out deer stalking again.

Ryan turned his thoughts to Stuart Brodie. He knew that he wasn't telling the whole truth. He obviously had a few skeletons in the closet, but then who didn't?

Ryan thought briefly about his own skeleton in the closet. This was something that he didn't like to do, for every time he did, the guilt seemed to get stronger.

No, Ryan thought, if Stuart Brodie has skeletons in the closet, then they are probably best kept there. He would have to live with them for the rest of his life as Ryan had to live with his own. Perhaps they could confess to each other, but Ryan knew that neither he nor Stuart would ever do that. That's why they are called skeletons in the closet.

Ryan was about ten miles from the Braes of Brackie Hotel when he noticed the blue 4 x 4 on his tail. Ryan suspected that they might be following him. From the little that Ryan could see, there seemed to be two people in the vehicle. The vehicle kept an even speed and a distance of about half a mile behind him.

Five miles further on, Ryan pulled into a garage to fill up with petrol, not that he actually needed much. The 4 x 4 kept on going. Neither the driver nor the passenger looked in towards the garage. This made Ryan suspicious, for most people, or at least the passenger, on a quiet country road would normally have a glanced in his direction.

Ryan took a note of the registration number as it passed. The 4x4 fitted the same description as the vehicle seen around the time of the crash that killed Sharon. But then surely, if that vehicle was the one that ran Sharon's car off the road, the local police would have caught up with it by now?

Ryan continued his journey and eventually pulled into the car park behind the Braes of Brackie Hotel. He glanced in his mirror. The blue 4x4 was there again. Ryan thought to himself was it just coincidence or was it a definite tail? He opted for the latter.

Before getting out of the car, Ryan phoned the traffic department with the registration of the 4x4. A few minutes later, a reply came back. The vehicle belonged to a company called West Coast fishing Industries Ltd. The company was owned by the late Gerald Bowman.

Ryan tried to fit the pieces together, Gerald Bowman was a victim of a drug-related murder and now Ryan was being tailed by a vehicles belonging to a company owned by the late Gerald Bowman. Does that mean that Bowman despite his clean record was involved in drugs? "Probably" thought Ryan. And, if this vehicle is the same vehicle that ran Sharon's car off the road causing her death, then is Ryan himself now a target? Getting too close perhaps? "Damn!" Ryan said aloud.

Another worrying thought came to Ryan; there must have been a lookout at the airport. How else would they know what type of car he had rented? But how did they know he was on his way back from London, let alone which flight he would be on? Ryan thought hard for a moment, and then it came to him when he phoned the Braes of Brackie Hotel to make a reservation the receptionist had asked him what time he expected to arrive at the hotel. Ryan had innocently told her which flight he was on and that he would probably arrive some two hours later. As this was the normal enough question for a receptionist to ask. Ryan had thought nothing of it at the time. He had thought that the receptionist was just being polite. However it seemed that the receptionist had passed the information on, what didn't make much sense was if there was an in-house spy, then why send out the goons? Unless of course they want it known, maybe a frightener, we're on to you, so watch your back.

Ryan was pissed-off that his cover was blown, but he was more annoyed at himself for not thinking things out a bit more. He now realised that he should have booked into a different hotel. The last thing that Ryan wanted was having a tail wherever he went. He hoped his backup would arrive soon.

Ryan shouldered his bag and walked up the steps to the reception, taking in the grandeur of the place. It filled him with a feeling of awe, the same feeling that he had on his first visit to the hotel. Nothing had changed, apart from the receptionist. Ryan didn't recognise her.

"Hello, how can I help you?" enquired the very smart lady behind the desk.

"Hi, I believe I spoke with you earlier on today regarding a reservation."

"Ah yes, you must be D.S, Jones."

Got you, thought Ryan, for he distinctly remembered not mentioning the 'D.S.' part when he booked the room, "That's right; you've got a good memory."

"Yes I have, if you could just sign here for me Mr Jones. I have given you room number nine, it's on the left at the top of the stairs, first floor. Will you be staying with us for long?"

"I am not quite sure, as I plan to do a bit of sight-seeing. I would imagine it will probably be for a few days at least, if that's okay."

"That's not a problem Mr Jones. You are welcome to stay for as long as you like. If you could just let me know in advance of your departure, so that I can make out your bill. If there is anything that I can do for you don't hesitate to ask and I hope that you enjoy your stay with us."

"Thank you, that's very kind of you." said Ryan as he picked up his room key. He had seen and heard enough to recognise a plant when he saw one.

"Dinner will be served in the dining room until ten pm. And breakfast is between six thirty and ten. Have a pleasant evening Mr Jones."

"Thank you I will. By the way, I notice you are not wearing a name badge."

"I am sorry. My name is Jill. I haven't got a badge yet as I only started a few days ago. It seems that I am the only 'Jill' that's ever worked here, so they're having one made for me."

"So tell me Jill, do come from around here?" said Ryan thinking, what the hell. After all, the best way to gain information was to play their game. By letting them think they have the upper hand, if played properly unknowingly to them, they give out more information than they receive.

"No I come from Glasgow actually. I felt like a break from the city, saw this job advertised and here I am."

"You surely don't drive to and from Glasgow every day do you?"

"Good heavens no, I have rented a small cottage just outside the village."

"Well I don't think you could have found a more peaceful and pleasant location than here Jill. I was here on business not so long ago. I really liked the area. I have some holidays to take, so I thought it would be quite nice to come back for a few days and see a bit more of the countryside. Maybe if you have any time off we could check it out together"

"Why Mr Jones that would be very nice, I will check the roster tomorrow and see what day I am off this week."

"Great and please, call me Ryan."

"Okay. Have a pleasant evening Ryan."

"You too Jill." said Ryan, returning Jill's flirtatious smile.

26

Stuart, after a fruitful day stalking arrived back that night a bit later than normal, he was very surprised and yet pleased to find Ryan Jones sitting by the fire in the lounge.

"Hello Ryan. You weren't away for long. Missed the place a bit too much did you?"

"Hello Stuart. Yes you might be right. Just a pity it's business and not pleasure. Still, I have to admit it is nice to be back."

"So how was your trip to London?"

"It went rather well. I had a good talk with my governor and told him about everything that's been going on. Tell me Stuart, have you seen a blue 4x4 about at all"

"Can't say that I have why do you ask?"

"I was followed by one most of the way back here, maybe it is the four by four that ran Sharon off the road, I am suspicious about her death and I am getting no information out of Glasgow police, they won't even tell me what Forensics found." Ryan sounded frustrated. "Anyway, tell me, how was your day Stuart?"

"My day has been quite good. I spent most of it at the Big Wood. I shot a couple of stags, and I might as well tell you I wasn't alone in the wood today. Although I didn't see him, I am certain it Russell was there"

"Bloody hell, are you sure?"

"Yes, pretty sure, there's nobody else I know that can be that evasive.

"So what do you think he's up to? If he didn't approach you, then what do you think he was doing in the wood?"

"I don't know. Maybe he's looking for a place to hide out, or trying to scare me. Maybe he's just letting me know that he's about. Either way, I don't like the thought of Russell creeping about and yes he does scare me. I don't know what he's up to. But, I do have some news; yesterday I met Steve in the wood. You remember Steve the big guy with the long hair and beard. You met him in here the same time that you met me."

"How could I forget him? Not only did he look like he was straight from the mountains, he looked like a bloody mountain."

"Anyway he was collecting firewood and I asked him if he had seen anyone else in the wood. He told me that he had met a person who claims to be carrying out plant research. Steve got talking to the guy and the guy told him that he had seen me about with my rifle."

"Do you know who he is?"

"Yes, Steve told me that he was staying at the Braes of Brackie Hotel. Steve couldn't remember his name. All he remembered was that he said he was a doctor, so I asked at the reception about him in a discreet way and guess what his name is?"

"Dr Livingston?"

"No, Dr Russell and the weird thing is, nobody ever actually sees him. He doesn't eat or drink here. All he does is sleep here."

"Bloody hell Stuart, you don't think that it could be Russell Hodges do you?"

"No, I think it's probably just coincidental that his name is Russell. I don't think that he would risk staying under the same roof as us, not under his own name anyway, or part of it"

"Maybe that's the way he would want you to think"

"Perhaps"

"If we can get the registration of his vehicle, I can run a check on it."

"I noted down the registration of all the cars in the car park, since you are back maybe you can check up on them, see if any are registered to a Dr Russell" asked Stuart

"Good idea, Stuart" Ryan assented "I'll give my guys in London a call. So Steve is the only person who has seen and talked to this guy?"

"As far as I know"

"Did Steve mention anything else about this Dr Russell?" asked Ryan.

"That's the other thing that made me wonder about Dr. Russell. He told Steve that he had permission from the owners. I checked with the Factor and he knows nothing about this Dr Russell."

"But you just said that he had permission from the owners, not the Factor."

"Yes I know, but if the owners did give this guy permission to carry out some kind of research, they should have informed the Factor about it. Everything that happens on the estate goes through the Factor."

"Who are the owners of the estate?" Ryan hadn't thought of this angle before.

"The Bellingham's, but they're never here. They're usually either in Switzerland or in Italy. So that means that our Dr. Russell might well have met them in Switzerland or Italy"

"You're becoming quite a detective Stuart. Tell me, do you know the Bellingham's first names?"

"Jason and Rachael, why?"

The expression on D.S. Ryan Jones's face changed to one of shock. Stuart was taken aback "Is everything alright Ryan? You look as if you have just seen a ghost."

"Yes fine, I have just remembered that I was supposed to make an important phone call, but it can keep till later" said Ryan.

Stuart was unconvinced but continued his story "I asked Steve about the Factor's farm and Steve said that the Factor lets part of the farm to a meat distribution company. The Factor does buy a lot of venison from the estate, right enough. Steve reckons this is a nice little sideline for the Factor."

"Ah" said Jones "Maybe there is something going on there sells the venison to himself at very low cost perhaps?"

"I don't think so" said Stuart "Steve told me the price which seems very fair. The estate gets the money fast, usually cash and there is no need to worry about selling or distributing the venison. On paper it would be a good deal for the estate" explained Stuart "Still I suppose there might be some scam going on. It would surprise me though the Factor seems such an upright man"

"Appearances can be deceptive, Stuart"

"I suppose" replied Stuart unconvinced.

"I don't suppose he gave you the name of the butcher did he?" asked Ryan.

"No, but what he did tell me, was that he met one of the drivers at the pub a few times. According to Steve the driver was a rough sort from Glasgow"

There was a silence between them, which was broken by the sound of high heels clicking as they approached. The sudden distraction gained both of their attention. "Sorry to interrupt you gentlemen. Ryan, I have just found out that my day off this week is Wednesday. Is that a good day for you?"

"Sure, Wednesday is fine by me. I will look forward to it."

"Great, shall I meet you at the reception after breakfast?"

"Why not? Let's get an early start and make a day of it. Would you care to join us for a drink?"

"No thanks, I have still some unpacking to do."

"Okay, I will see you on Thursday morning then, Jill."

"Goodnight." said Jill, giving Ryan an even more exaggerated flirtatious smile than before.

"Bloody hell Ryan, you don't waste much time do you?" exclaimed Stuart the minute Jill had turned away.

"I will talk to you about her later; you know what I think Stuart?"

"What?"

"I think we have discovered how the drug ring operates.

27

Ryan began to explain with Stuart listening intently.

"There is a fortified farm housing rare sheep that need rare feed. There is a fishing business that does little fishing but does bring in from Ireland the sheep feed. There are butcher vans picking up deer carcasses and distributing though-out the West of Scotland."

"Okay" Stuart nodded beginning to understand where Ryan was going with this.

"So the drugs arrive as sheep feed and the drugs are distributed in the Butcher vans. It's almost perfect. What better way than in meat vans? No-one would suspect them, even if they were stopped and checked. Drugs hidden amongst meat would be hard to detect, especially if the vans are chilled which they probably are. Quite a clever set up don't you think?"

"Yes it certainly is"

"Caledonian Land Holdings is likely a front to launder the drug money, with one of the money laundering method the cash purchase of the deer carcases. And, I am sorry to say that your Factor is likely up to his neck in this. You know he called in a favour from the head of Glasgow C.I.D to have me taken of the case. It is his farm and he was involved with Caledonian Land Holdings. He must be one of the ring leaders"

Stuart had to agree, much as he liked and respected Peter Grant there was no other explanation. If Ryan's theory was correct, then the Factor was a drug runner and probably high on Russell's hit-list. "What is your plan, Ryan" asked Stuart "Well, I have been ordered not to do anything drastic until I get back-up. So, meantime, I am going to find out more about that land-buying company. At the same time I have to keep a low profile, even more so now, since I was followed today. I wouldn't mind however, going stalking with you tomorrow if that's okay. It will help to clear my head"

"Sure, if you want. Just remember that Russell might be lurking about or maybe even two of them."

"That's okay. I'll take my chance and like you said, if Russell was going to take either of us out, he would have done so by now. Besides, you're the one with the gun" said Ryan with a touch more bravado than he actually felt. But, he had a job to do Russell Hodges had to be stopped.

Stuart decided it was time to lighten the atmosphere he decided to have some fun at the expense of Ryan's new romance "Now, you were going to tell me about what's her name? Ah yes, the delectable Jill"

"The delectable Jill, as you put it, is a plant, or should I say a spy" Ryan informed Stuart

"What! For whom?" Stuart was taken aback.

"The Factor of course" said Ryan with certainty

"But how do you know?" Stuart was unconvinced.

"Because she is the only person here in Scotland that knew which flight I was arriving on. When I made the booking for the room she asked me what time I expected to arrive at and I stupidly told her the time of the flight."

"But how does that make her a spy?"

"I told you earlier, I was followed from the airport to the hotel."

"But that doesn't really make sense Ryan. Why follow you if they already knew where you were going?"

"It makes sense if they want you to know that they are following you; a tactic to try and scare you off. Besides it's the easiest bit of skirt I have ever pulled. She's probably been told to come on to me and try and get what information she can"

"And you're going to go along with it?" Stuart was surprised that Ryan would take the chance.

"Absolutely, after all I am the detective. I know more about the game she's playing than she does and I will bet you anything you like that the delectable Jill is staying in the same cottage that Sharon stayed in."

"I suppose you'll do whatever you have to do, in the line of duty of course" was Stuart's wry response.

"Perish the thought old boy. I never mix business with pleasure" responded Ryan with a smirk.

"Well I bloody would given half a chance with her". Stuart was a bit jealous and he had to admit that Jill hadn't given him a second look "You know" he said to Ryan "There is something about her. I just can't put my finger on it, I am sure I've seen her somewhere before, but I just can't think where."

"Yes, probably in your dreams Stuart" Ryan joked "Now how about another drink?"

The object of their conversation had just reached her new home. It was indeed Sharon's cottage that Jill now rented. Jill changed into a lace and satin nightdress and poured herself a drink. There came a knock at the door. Jill opened the door in her revealing outfit.

"I was beginning to think you weren't coming"

"Sorry I got delayed at the farm, how did the plan go?"

"Hook line and sinker."

"So it's arranged for Friday then?"

"Yes, he didn't hesitate."

"Good, I will let you know the details nearer the time. The sooner that D.S Jones is out of the way the better. He's getting too close to Stuart Brodie for my liking and you're sure Brodie didn't recognise you?"

"Yes I am quite sure, it was a long time ago even then we didn't actually meet properly."

"You're a very clever girl Jill."

"That's why you pay me so well Peter. Now come on, bed, we've lost time to make up."

In their haste, on entering the bedroom, the Factor tripped over a box.

"Bloody hell, I told Sharon's sister to come and clear all of this stuff out of here"

"Never mind about that just now Peter. Get your clothes off."

28

Ryan and Stuart parted company for the night at a little after nine thirty. Both made their way to their own rooms. Ryan sat on his bed and made the supposed important phone call, the one that he told Stuart he had forgotten about.

"Hi Guv, it's Ryan Jones."

"Hello Ryan is everything alright?"

"I am not quite sure yet."

"Why what has happened?"

"Nothing as such but I have just found out who the owners of this estate are."

"The one that this Factor and Brodie are on?"

"Yes. The owners are Jason and Rachael Bellingham."

"Are you sure about this Ryan?"

"Positive unless there's another couple with identical names."

"Christ, if it is them, then it could be a completely different ball game."

"How the hell did Jason Bellingham end up owning a bloody estate in Scotland?"

"Apparently he was the nearest male relative of the previous owner and he inherited the estate when he died."

"Some people have all the bloody luck, mind you; he wasn't so lucky the last time, when you were on his case Ryan."

"No, he wasn't but then he only got five years. It should have been twenty five." "Right, here's what to do Ryan. Just carry on as planned and I will see what I can find out about Bellingham's present activities. Interpol must surely be keeping tabs on him, especially after what he did. Do you know if they live on the estate?"

"No, they hardly ever come here. They either live in Switzerland or Italy."

"Yes, well that figures doesn't it?" replied Paul King.

"They might all be in this together you know; the Factor, Bellingham and Stuart Brodie."

"I thought you said that you trusted Brodie?"

"I do in a way, but he is very smart and he might just be leading me up the garden path."

"Okay, listen, if Jason Bellingham is involved, you better be careful, because if he finds out that you are on to him again, he might resume the contract on you."

"Yes I know. I have already thought about that Sir"

"Just watch your back Ryan and I will get back to you as soon as, ok?"

"I certainly will don't worry Guv."

Ryan switched off his mobile and threw it onto the bed.   He lay back with his hands behind his head and shut his eyes. The ordeal from five years ago came flooding back.

29

Ryan and Stuart met in the hotel foyer as arranged at four thirty in the morning.

"Good morning Ryan."

"Good morning Stuart. It looks another fine morning"

"Yes it does and let's hope it stays that way for the forecast is rain spreading in from the west at some point hopefully we'll have been and gone by then."

"I was thinking during the night Stuart."

"I bet you were."

"About the Factor's farm"

"Sorry, I thought it might have been about your hot date on Thursday."

"No, she's the last thing on my mind. I maybe shouldn't ask you, but do you think we could possibly go out to the farm for a look?"

"I thought you said the place was like fort Knox."

"It is, but there are some high hills nearby. If we could get to the top of one of the hills, with your binoculars we could get quite a good view of the farm buildings and maybe see what's going on, what do you think?"

"I don't know Ryan, it's a bit risky. If we were caught, well for one thing I would lose my job, house the lot. Oh, what the hell! The way things are going, I might lose them anyway. Okay I have some maps of this area in the Land Rover. The only problem I have is, I can't take my rifle onto someone else's land and I won't leave it in the Land Rover, so we'll leave it here." Stuart removed the middle cushion in the front of the Land Rover and lifted the steel plate to reveal a box compartment. Inside were all sorts of things as well as a bundle of maps. Stuart sifted through them until he found the right one for the area.

"Okay, now let's see. We are here, where do you think the Factor's farm is?"

"I reckon this is the road up to it, here." said Ryan who indicated with his finger on the map. "As you can see, there is only one way in and out to the farm. Looking at the contour lines of the hills on the map, you can see how close and high they are."

"That's not what's bothering me, what's bothering me is where do we park the Land Rover?"

Ryan was going to make a suggestion that they take his car, but decided not to as he realised they knew what type of car he was driving. Stuart studied the map for several minutes.

"If we drive up this road here for three or four miles and park round about here then walk due west up over these hills it will bring us to here, which will be a good vantage point. It will take maybe three hours or so, maybe even longer. I don't know for I have never been on these hills and I don't know what the terrain is like.   So, if you think you're up to it, that's what we'll do."

"That's fine by me let's go."

"I just hope you're a bit fitter than the last time we went out on the hills." said Stuart with a knowing smile.

"Don't worry about me Stuart I'll be fine."

Ryan felt a little bit annoyed that Stuart had noticed how unfit he had been on their last outing.

Stuart had driven five or six miles from the hotel when they passed the same 4 x 4 that had tailed Ryan the day before, parked in a lay-by. Ryan brought this to Stuart's attention. It was early in the morning and still quite dark, so they couldn't make out who or how many people were in the vehicle. They would find that out later in the day.

Ryan glanced back at the 4x4 after they had passed. He half-expected it to follow them, but then he realised, why should it? They weren't to know that he was travelling in Stuart Brodie's Land Rover. Then again, there was always the possibility that they might be watching Stuart as well, for the Factor must surely have been informed by now about their relationship. Ryan had another quick glance behind. The 4x4 was still stationary.

"Don't worry Ryan, it's not following us."

"Yes I know, just making sure."

"You seem a little bit jumpy this morning. Is everything alright?"

"Yes, everything's fine. I've just got a feeling that things aren't quite right."

"What, you mean like a gut feeling?"

"Something like that, maybe I've just been in the police force for too long."

"Never mind Ryan, a good long hike will help to clear your head. I know it certainly works for me."

"You are probably right Stuart, I am worrying about nothing. A good long walk is what I need."

Half a mile further along the road, they reached the turn-off for the road they intended to drive up.

"Damn!" said Ryan, for across the road was an iron gate with a chain and padlock around it. Stuart stopped the Land Rover in front of the gate and fished out a key from the metal box under the middle seat and handed it to Ryan.

"How come?" said Ryan with a look of surprise.

"There's a disused quarry at the end of this road where the locals do their clay target shooting and I used to come up some times, so they gave me a key."

"Nice one" said Ryan

As he got out of the Land Rover to open the gate, Ryan remembered he had some information for Stuart, "Oh by the way Stuart, I checked out those registration numbers you gave me"

"Oh yes, any luck?"

"Nothing, none of the cars are registered to Dr Russell or hired to a Dr Russell. So either his name is not Russell or he doesn't have a car"

"I can't believe he doesn't have a car" said Stuart confused.

"Maybe he was out in it, when you took the numbers?" suggested Ryan.

"No" Stuart shook his head "I keep checking the car park for any new cars. I gave you the numbers of all the cars parked at the hotel over the last few days"

"Well this is curious, the elusive Dr Russell I wonder who he really is?"

30

The road to the quarry was not much more than a single track, it was over-grown in places with broom and birch saplings. It had originally been constructed of quarry stone and whin dust but with the lack of traffic on it, the road surface had become very soft for driving on. In addition the lack of compaction meant that any vehicle or creature heavy enough would leave a well defined imprint.

After driving for about a mile Stuart parked the Land Rover at the side of the track amongst the broom and birch trees. He wasn't deliberately trying to hide the Land Rover; he parked of the track in case another vehicle came along this way the other vehicle could pass. He wanted to leave the access open.

The terrain over the hills was better for walking than Stuart thought it would be. They reached the top of a heavily wooded hill to the east of the farm in just two hours. From where they were seated, just below the horizon, they had a perfect view of the entire farm and of the road which led into it. Stuart focused his binoculars and handed them to Ryan. Stuart was long-sighted and so didn't need them he could make out almost every detail about the farm except for one thing that was covered-over with a green tarpaulin.

"Ryan, do you see the two A.T.V.s?"

"Yes" responded Ryan.

"Can you make out what's under the tarpaulin next to them?" queried Stuart.

"Bloody hell Stuart, it's a fucking helicopter. There was me thinking how stupid they were for only having one road in. With the C.C.T.V. they have at the gate keeping an eye on the road, by the time anyone broke through the gate, they would be out the back door and long gone" exclaimed Ryan in shock.

"And those A.T.Vs are tracked machines, they could climb over these hills in no time at all, with the main men escaping in the 'copter" Stuart explained.

"That is no doubt the escape plan but they won't get away Stuart, not if I have my way, because I will make sure there's a police helicopter in on the raid. Christ, it's just as well that we came here for a look, otherwise we would have just barged our way through the front gate. Okay, we might get the basket of eggs, so to speak, but the chickens would have flown the coop."

"Maybe we could get Russell to sit here with a sniper's rifle and shoot them as they come out" Stuart suggested.

"Or maybe you Stuart"

"That's not my line of work Ryan."

"No, you're right Stuart, it's not your line of work, but if it was, do you think you would be able to shoot someone at this distance? I have seen you use your rifle remember, I know how good a shot you are."

"Yes if it was my job and I had to."

Silence fell between them, as they both stared down towards the farm, surveying the scene. Stuart's thoughts were focussed on what Ryan had just asked him. So were Ryan's.

Ten minutes passed before the silence was broken. "Tell me about Rick Maynard Stuart, what happened to him? How did he die?"

Stuart paused for a few moments, looking straight into Ryan's eyes, wondering whether to tell him the truth.

"Russell and I were in this restaurant one night, having a meal and a quiet drink. Rick came in with his girl friend. He spotted us and came over to our table, then started ranting. He accused me of being a traitor and that I had better watch my back. He said that he didn't like the company I was keeping. Russell told him it was he that should watch his back. Rick then went and sat at a table near the far end of the restaurant, which just happened to be next to a fire exit. Russell and I finished our drinks and left. When we went out to the car park, Rick was waiting for us. The car park was quiet and secluded, with lots of trees about. Rick started ranting again, only this time it was directed more towards Russell."

"What was he ranting on about?" Ryan quizzed Stuart.

Stuart replied "Rick was saying things like Russell shouldn't stick his nose in where it doesn't belong and that he made a big mistake in taking me away from him. He told Russell that his days were numbered, in fact he said both ours were. Russell told him that he didn't know what he was talking about and that he should be careful with his threats. The next thing that happened, Rick seemed to blow a fuse. He made a lunge for Russell, but he never stood a chance."

"Why what happened next?" asked Ryan.

"Russell pulled out a gun and shot him right between the eyes and that was the end of Rick."

"So then what happened?"

"We got in Russell's car and out of there as quick as we could. He then dropped me off at my flat. A few hours later the police arrived and I think you know the rest."

"What about Russell's cousin, David Philips, how well did you know him?"

"Not very well, I only met him a few times he seemed a reasonable sort of guy. I think he was into sourcing electronic parts or something for companies back in America. Why all the questions? I am beginning to feel like I am being interrogated" Stuart was feeling uncomfortable worried he had said too much he had never told anyone about Russell and Rick before.

"Just curious that's all and I think you did the right thing, getting out of there when you did. Obviously Russell doesn't hold a grudge against you, because like you said, if he did he would have sorted you out by now, but that doesn't excuse him for what he is and somehow he has to be stopped."

"Yes I know, even although I like the guy, you're right, but it isn't going to be easy" agreed Stuart.

"Have you ever killed anyone Stuart?"

"What do you think?"

"I think you have"

"There's not much point in me answering your question then, is there?" was Stuart's cold reply.

"Probably not I don't suppose you would tell me anyway even if you had" asserted Ryan.

"Do you actually think anyone in their right mind would?" Stuart was a bit pissed-off now, Ryan was pushing too hard.

"As a matter of fact I do. Sometimes murderers actually want to be caught"

"The thing is Ryan, is the murderer in the right frame of mind to start with?"

"That's a question for the psychiatrists. What I am trying to say is that, eventually their conscience gets the better of them. The burden of guilt becomes so heavy that they can't live with it. I know there are all types of killers, but I am talking about murderers in general, the ones that kill on impulse or even those that commit premeditated murders."

"What about soldiers, where do they fit in?"

"Now I think that's a bit different Stuart."

"Why?"

"Well for a start they are professionally trained to protect us, against terrorists and the like."

"Russell Hodges was professionally trained by the army."

"But he's not in the army now is he?"

"No, but he's still trying to protect the nation, by killing drug dealers."

"That might be so Stuart, the only thing wrong with what he's doing is he's killing civilians. That is cold-blooded murder, totally the opposite of fighting a war."

"What about the war against drugs?"

"I understand what you are trying to say here Stuart. All I can say is that Hodges is in the U.K murdering civilians and it is my duty to stop him."

Ryan and Stuart stared hard at each other, neither willing to back down.

"So, tell me Ryan, have you ever killed anyone?"

"No, I can honestly say that I have not."

"Could you?"

"It would all depend on the circumstances and I just hope that I am never in a situation where I have to."

"In that case, I hope that you never come up against Russell Hodges, because believe me, he won't hesitate to kill you if he has to."

"That maybe so, but like I said, it would all depend on the circumstances. Now, I think we should change the subject, don't you?"

"Yes, I agree with you there."

Ryan now wished that he had never asked Stuart if he had ever killed someone. The last thing that he wanted was for them to fall out; besides, he had a feeling he already knew the answer to that question. Best to let sleeping dogs lie.

31

Ryan and Stuart were about to start hiking their way back to the land rover when the saw a blue transit van drive up to the farm gate. A man got out of the passenger's side of the van and walked over to the intercom. He stood there for a few seconds before the gate slid open. Ryan turned to Stuart "This could be part of the set-up, these guys might be the couriers" The van passed through the gateway the gate automatically slid back into place.

There was no writing or any other marking on the van. Ryan read out the registration number and Stuart wrote it down in his diary. Before the van reached the farm yard, a sliding door opened on the largest building. Two men stepped outside. They were wearing white overalls, the type that crime-scene officers wear. The transit van reversed inside the building, the two men followed and the sliding door closed.

"I think we've seen enough Stuart, to know how they operate. I will check out that registration when we get back find out who the van belongs to"

"I wonder how long this little operation's been going on. Who would have thought? Right here, in the highlands of Scotland" wondered Stuart

"Quite some time I expect and it's anything but little. As to the location, well it's perfect for what they're up to, very secluded and private. The rare sheep thing's a perfect excuse to keep unwanted visitors out. We had a similar case in Wales several years ago, but instead of rare sheep it was rare pigs they used as a cover. They didn't however distribute the drugs under the pretence of meat deliveries. No, this is a far bigger set up and a very clever one at that. Your Factor's a very smart man and probably a very rich one at that, but not for much longer" responded Ryan grimly.

Stuart and Ryan cautiously began the two hour hike back to the Land Rover. There was to be no more talk about murders or murderers, at least not for the time being anyway, just companionable silence.

When they arrived at the Land Rover, Stuart and Ryan had a bite to eat. It was almost midday.

"So what's the plan for the rest of the day Stuart?"

"I was thinking of returning to collect my rifle and heading over to the big wood. Do you want to come or have you done enough walking for one day?"

"Sure I would like to come if you don't mind my company that is?"

"Not at all Ryan, I be glad of the extra pair of eyes"

After their quick lunch, Stuart turned the Land Rover and started to drive down the track. He hadn't gone more than fifty yards when he stopped, noticing that there were new tyre tracks on top of the land rover tracks.

"What's the matter Stuart?"

"Look at the tyre tracks on the road. Someone followed us up here. Whoever it was has deliberately kept within our tracks and this is as far as they came. You can see where the overlaid tracks stop."

They both got out of the Land Rover for a closer inspection. After looking closely at the tyre imprints for a few minutes, Ryan reasoned "The tracks are almost the same width as the Land Rovers, but the tread is road tyres, not off-road like the land rover. The vehicle is about the same size, although not as heavy. A large car or van I would say."

"Tell you what Ryan, if you wait here, I will take the Land Rover back to where we parked it. You stand where the other car stopped. I will check if I can see you"

"Good idea Stuart."

Stuart turned the Land Rover around and parked in exactly the same place as before. After a few minutes, he drove back to where Ryan was.

"Well?" asked Ryan

"I couldn't see you so the car could have been here the driver spying on us while we were spying on the farm" Stuart was worried.

"This seems a bit risky we could have turned around at any point to come back down" said Ryan "And how did they get back down the track without turning round"

"That's easy" grinned Stuart.

"They reversed of course" said Ryan and Stuart in unison and they laughed breaking the tension.

"It's all food for thought Stuart. That's the interesting thing about detective work you're always prepared for the unexpected and in most cases, that's the way it is"

"Okay we better get going. We're wasting time" decided Stuart.

Stopped the Land Rover in front of the gate Ryan got out to unlock it. The padlock was the type where you need to turn the key to lock, as well as to unlock. But when Ryan took hold of the padlock which had appeared locked to Ryan's surprise, the padlock fell open it had been unlocked all the time.

Climbing back into the Land Rover, Ryan turned, looked at Stuart and shook his head.

"What's the matter now?" said Stuart

"The padlock was open and I know I locked it behind us" replied Ryan

"So? Whoever was followed us couldn't be bothered to lock it properly, or was in too big of a rush" speculated Stuart.

"Or maybe they didn't have a key." said Ryan raising his eyebrows. They were both quiet for the next mile or so.

Ryan spoke first "Who do you know that's capable of picking a lock like that?"

"You know as well as I do." said Stuart.

Suppose he had followed them out onto the hill and crept up close enough to hear their conversation. If Russell has heard me telling Ryan about Asia he will be far from happy, though a very worried Stuart.

Stuart turned to Ryan "If it was Russell he didn't do much of a job of hiding the fact he had followed us, maybe it wasn't Russell, maybe it was the two guys that are following you"

"I don't think so Stuart" said Ryan "I don't think they are that smart"

A few miles later they passed lay-by where the blue 4 x 4 had been parked this morning. It was still there but it was now cordoned-off with police crime-scene tape, no one was about. Stuart slowed down.

"Pull over Stuart. Let's have a look" instructed Ryan.

Stuart parked the Land Rover on the verge next to the lay-by. Ryan and Stuart got out and closely inspected the 4x4. It looked like the vehicle had been in an accident recently, although it had bull bars fitted at the front, they were dented and as Ryan looked closer he could see traces of red paint.

"Can you remember what colour Sharon's car was?" Ryan asked Stuart.

"It was red the same colour as that paint" responded Stuart "It looks like the police have finally found the car. I am surprised it took them so long"

Ryan peered in a side window "I don't think that's the reason Stuart there is blood on both of the front seats. I think this is another murder. We must assume the worst, but who and why?"

"Maybe they have been killed in retaliation for killing Sharon killing and if so, all I can say is well done to the killer" Stuart smiled grimly "I will buy him a drink." Stuart felt no pity for the people who had died in the 4x4. He was glad if Sharon's death had been avenged.

32

When Stuart and Ryan arrived back at the hotel, they found a police reception waiting for them.

"I don't know how you managed to get your superior to agree to you coming back here, but be warned D.S. Jones, as far as I am concerned, you have no jurisdiction here whatsoever. In fact, if you interfere in our investigations at all, or withhold any information, I will have you arrested and the same goes for you Mr Brodie." said Superintendent Blake.

Blake was a tall slightly over-weight rather severe woman. She had short, dark hair, a ruddy complexion and large, protruding blue eyes.

Ryan replied smoothly "Nothing to do with police work actually. It just so happens I have a few days off and I thought it would be nice to see a bit more of Scotland. Stuart has been kind enough to take me out deer stalking. By the way, we passed a blue 4x4 in a lay-by. Is that the same one that was involved in the Sharon's hit and run accident?"

"Like I just said a minute ago, that is no concern of yours. Now if you will excuse me, I have work to do. Enjoy your holiday."

The superintendent marched out of foyer. She stopped outside the front door and turned to look back inside. As she did, she spoke to the other two policemen that were with her.

Stuart lip read and translated the conversation for Ryan. "Right you two; I want you to stick to Jones like shit on your shoe. I want to know everything that he does, where he goes and who he meets. I don't care if he knows that you're following him; just don't let him out of your sight okay? Now make sure you keep me informed."

"Well, we shall see about that Mrs high and mighty Blake. Thanks Stuart. It's a handy thing you being able to lip-read" commented Ryan.

"Yes it is, but sometimes you read things that you would rather not know about" observed Stuart.

Just at that moment the hotel Manager called out after Blake "Catherine"

Blake turned "Yes Gordon?"

"Thank goodness I caught you" said the manager "I wanted a word about the autumn meeting, It wont take long if you could come to the office?"

"OK" said Blake following him back in.

Ryan and Jones looked at each other in amazement "'Catherine', who would have thought it? It is too much of a coincidence if she is involved with Caledonia Land Holdings, then she is part of the drug ring" Ryan pointed out.

"It would explain how they have got away with it for so long" conceded Stuart loath to believe that the head of Glasgow C.I.D. was a drug runner but that's the way it appeared.

"Well Stuart after recent events I will have to pass on the stalking. I have too much work to be getting on with" Ryan said apologetically.

"Don't worry Ryan I understand" Stuart assured him.

They separated Stuart headed towards the gun room and Ryan to his own room. Once in his room Ryan phoned his boss straight away.

"Hello Chief, Ryan Jones.

"Hello Ryan, how are things going up there in bonnie Scotland?" replied Paul King.

"Well a few more things have come to light. First point is I am certain that the drugs are stored at the Factor's farm. I had a look at the place through binoculars today. There is even a bloody helicopter and A.T.V's for a quick getaway in case of a raid."

"Do we know how they are moving the drugs?" asked King.

"I think so. My theory is that the drugs are brought into the local harbour on fishing boats concealed in animal feed bags. From there they are loaded onto the Factor's lorry and taken to his farm. The drugs are then distributed in meat delivery vans. I don't have their company name yet. But while we were observing the farm today, I think we saw one of the vans arrive I noted the registration."

"So you were not alone?" said King picking up on the use of 'we'.

"I was with Stuart Brodie. He took me out in his Land Rover. We hiked over the hills to where I could get a better view of the farm" explained Ryan.

"So you've got yourself a new partner then?"

"He's just helping me out."

"Okay, but I thought you said you weren't sure if you could trust him."

"I do now and I am 100% sure the Factor's our man, unless of course if some evidence comes up that Jason Bellingham is directly involved."

"Nothing has come back to me yet about Bellingham, but I wouldn't rule him out yet" instructed King.

"Don't worry I'm not" agreed Ryan "He is the owner of the estate and the Factor works for him, possibly in more ways than one"

"Maybe we should hold back until we know if Bellingham is directly involved, because if he is, it would be bloody nice to nail him again" suggested King.

"Yes I know it would Guv, but even if he is, it won't be easy nailing him this time, especially if he is living in Switzerland or Italy."

"If we can get some hard evidence, then we will go and get the bastard Ryan."

"I think the only way we are going to find out if Bellingham is involved, is when we nail the Factor and the Factor grasses on him."

"You're probably right. Good work Ryan and what about the land-buying company?"

"Again the Factor is involved the company rented an office on his farm. I have my boys digging up all they can on Caledonian Land Holdings, I am sure we will find a link"

Ryan changed tack "Do you remember the woman that was killed in the hit-and-run a few days ago?"

"Yes, she worked at the hotel where you are staying didn't she?"

"Yes and the vehicle that ran her off the road was a blue 4x4. Well it tailed me to the hotel yesterday. On our way to the Factor's farm this morning, it was parked in a lay-by. It was still there this afternoon, only this time it was cordoned-off with police tape. Going by the damage to the front and the paint marks on it, I would say it's it a good fit for the car that ran Sharon off the road. But, there was blood stains on the front seats" Ryan quickly recapped.

"What do you think has happened Ryan?"

"I reckon that the Factor had Sharon killed to stop her talking. They'd had an affair in the past not long after her husband was killed in a fishing accident. The husband worked for the fishing company that I think is smuggling in the drugs. As to who killed the men in the 4x4 I don't know, maybe it was a drug revenge killing or maybe it was

Hodges which would fit if the men worked for the Factor and were involved in the drug ring. I also suspect that Superintendent Blake."

"Blake, my goodness that is a serious allegation Ryan" King sounded worried.

"Sharon mentioned that the other person involved with Gerald Bowman and the Factor in Caledonian Land Holdings was called Catherine. And what is Blake's first name? Catherine. Not only that but Blake was waiting for me at the hotel when I got back and she was not very happy. She told me that she couldn't understand why you let me come back. I told her that I had a few days off."

"Good."

"Then the bitch gave me a very stern warning to stay away from police business, as I had no jurisdiction here."

"Did she now?"

"Yes and she's left two of her men to keep an eye on me"

King thought for a moment and then gave Ryan his orders "OK Ryan. Try and give Blake's' men the slip and find yourself another place to stay. Check out that van you saw, find out who it belongs to and dig up as much as you can on that land company. Meantime, I will pass this info upstairs and as soon we decide we are ready to make the bust, I will let you know. We are on to a big one here Ryan and by the way, you are doing a bloody good job up there. Well done, keep your head down and I will be in touch."

"Okay Guv, the sooner the better."

33

Stuart made his way to the big wood. There was still enough daylight left in the day to try and catch up with a few beasts. Stuart had the need to get back into his own world. He had a lot on his mind, so many questions; was the Factor really the leader of a drug ring? How many more people were going to die? Who was the elusive Dr Russell? As to the future Stuart had no idea if he would he even have a job at the end of all this? Was Russell here in Scotland?

At least back in Asia he and Russell were on the same side and Stuart trusted Russell with his life. Stuart suspected that he could not trust Russell at all, let alone with his life. Now that Russell had started on this he had mad, killing spree but had he?

Stuart's intuition told him there was something not quite right with the picture Stuart knew what type of person Russell was, how his mind worked, how he operated. Sure, Stuart had no doubt that the killings were down to Russell, at the same time, it didn't seem to be Russell's style. Russell liked to move in for the kill as quick as possible, get the job done and away again. He would certainly not hang about afterwards in the way that he seems to be now. Why all the cat and mouse tactics?

Russell seemed to be deliberately letting his presence be known. Just like on the quarry road, with the tyre tracks and the padlock on the gate. Stuart knew that Russell could open and shut a padlock like that one in a matter of seconds.

Instead he pretends that he can't, or that he hasn't enough time to lock it properly, why? Is he just playing a game to torment and tease us? Because an attention-seeker is something Russell never was so why now. Maybe Russell was losing it, or as Ryan had theorized earlier, all murderers secretly would like to be caught.

Maybe it is not Russell, for Stuart hadn't seen him face to face, or had he? Some people can change their appearance quite easily, although Stuart had never known Russell to use a disguise in the past. He was so elusive that he didn't have to. Maybe, after all Russell is the mysterious Dr Russell, for Stuart hadn't seen him either.

It was all too much for Stuart to comprehend Stuart knew that there were drug dealers and murders committed in the cities. But this was in the Scottish highlands, right on his own doorstep, who would have thought it? And it has been going on for years and I had no idea thought Stuart and he felt very stupid.

Another point that puzzled Stuart was the lack of publicity. Stuart did not watch much television or read newspapers very often, but something like this should definitely be making the headlines every day. Even Sharon's death had been played down. Stuart recalled the time when there had been a spate of sheep-rustling. That had made headline news for weeks. Yet, here we were with drug murders up and down the country which the police knew were connected and yet hardly anything at all has been mentioned in the press.

Stuart wondered if the police were deliberately with-holding information from the media. It would fit if Superintendent Blake was involved, someone in her position could direct the media and press attention away from the murders. So following that train of thought the reason for the lack of press coverage could be that Blake doesn't want the press or media digging as she knows that she has too much to lose. It's not just money or her job that she could lose, it's also her life. She surely must have known that if she got involved in drug trafficking, that was it, there was no turning back.

Stuart understood how the system worked. To get out was a brave thing to do, or at least try. Unfortunately for most, greed got the better of them. Or in some cases it's fear, fear for their lives, that keeps them involved, but in Blake's case, Stuart reckoned that greed was the driving force.

There was still one question to be answered that off Russell's real motive? If in fact it is Russell, the Special Forces must have trained dozens just like him: loyal and courageous men who have served their countries for years killing the enemy, the type of men who find it hard to adjust to civilian life. They are after all, highly-trained killing machines.

Stuart had arrived at his destination without realising it. He had driven there as though he'd been on auto-pilot. Stuart switched off the Land Rover's engine, for he had now been sitting stationary for almost half an hour, pondering over his thoughts. "Who gives a fuck anyway? Shit happens!" said Stuart aloud as he slid out of the Land Rover, knowing that, frustration was getting the better of him.

Suddenly he spotted the three stags less than two hundred yards away, crossing the ride in front of him. This brought Stuart back to reality. The game was on. He was would go into stealth mode, this was his world and this is what he did best the deer were Stuart's enemy. They had to die.

It was well into the night before Stuart finished up in the Larder. The three red deer stags were now hanging lifeless. They no longer resembled deer, or any other animal. Hanging upside down from stainless steel hooks which were inserted between the Achilles' tendon and the bone, the bottom part of their hind legs had been removed.

Two cuts with a bone-saw had removed a section of bone from the inner pelvis, along with the penis or pizzal, a term used in the hunting fraternity, with testacies still attached. The pizzal was highly valued by the Chinese and Japanese. They dry them out and then grind them up into small pieces. The proceeds were then sold-on at very high prices as an aphrodisiac.

Further down the carcase, a plastic spacer holding open the rib cage which had been parted with a saw-cut down the centre of the breast bone. This enabled the carcase to cool down quicker and also helped in the removal of the heart, lungs and the trachea.

The bottom part of the legs from the knee down were also removed, along with the head., the carcasses were now ready to be up-lifted by the game dealer, or, as Stuart had recently discovered, Steve would collect them and take them to the Factor's farm and then, be used to conceal drugs. Even chilled venison still had a very strong smell about it, strong enough to throw any sniffer-dog off the scent.

The Factor was a smart man indeed.

34

By the time Stuart eventually returned to the Braes of
Brackie Hotel it was almost eleven o'clock at night. He
knew that he was too late for a meal in the restaurant, so it
was going to have to be room service. But, first he went to
put his rifle away in the gun room he caught sight of the
crowded noisy bar and was intrigued.

Stuart soon discovered what all the noise was about. It
was the A.G.M. of the Rare Sheep Breeders' Society. Stuart
had been at the hotel once before when they had held their
A.G.M. That had turned out to be quite entertaining, for the
members had all fallen-out with each other and started
fighting. To Stuart's surprise, the Factor was there. The
Factor noticed Stuart at the bar and headed over to him.

"Hello Stuart. You're late on the go tonight."

"Hello Peter. Yes I have just got back from the
Larder. I had three stags to take care of."

"Well done, that will be three less to worry about.
How are the fencers getting on? Did you speak to them
about the deer jumps?"

"They're getting on fine and no, I haven't spoken to
them about the deer jumps yet. I will go and see them
tomorrow"

"Okay, but make sure that you do because we don't
want them building them in the wrong places now do we?"

"Like I said, I will go and see them tomorrow. "I
would join you for a drink but I better get back to the

meeting, before they start falling out with each other" said the Factor with a wry smile.

"That's okay; I am just having a quick pint before I go up to my room. It's been a long day and I badly need a shower" Stuart smiled in response.

"Oh, there was just one other thing Stuart, I believe that you had some company today."

"Yes that's right. I took Ryan Jones out on the hills this morning. He's on holiday for a few days and wanted to see around about."

"Well I hardly think that's your responsibility, do you? Especially when you have your own job to do? Just suppose something should happen to him, if he was injured in an accident. The estate's insurance wouldn't cover him. In fact, we would more than likely be liable. So no more tour guides, okay?" instructed the Factor.

"Okay, that's fine by me" conceded Stuart not wanting to get into a discussion about exactly what he had been showing Jones.

"Right, I better go. Enjoy your pint and don't forget the fencers."

"I won't."

The Factor made his way back to the A.G.M. Stuart was glad to see the back of him, for he was starting to nip his head. Stuart thought how right Ryan was about the Factor and his spies.

Stuart finished his pint and headed upstairs. He had just turned towards his room at the top when Ryan came of his own room.

"Ah ha, just the very man. I was on my way to look for you" Ryan greeted Stuart.

"Hello Ryan, your room or mine?"

"Come into mine" replied Ryan.

Inside Ryan's room, Stuart noticed the packed hold-all on the bed. "Going somewhere?" Stuart asked.

"Yes. I am going to check out in the morning and find another place to stay. Do you know of any places nearby, that are maybe a little bit more secluded than here?"

"There are plenty of guest houses along the coast road. There's one just before you enter the next village, on the right hand side of the road. I can't remember what it's called, but it is set well-in off the main road, very secluded and private. Why, what's the problem?"

"I don't intend to be followed everywhere I go, so what I plan to do is check out of here, go and change my car for another and hopefully lose my followers during the process. Then I will come back and book into another place. That place you just mentioned sounds ideal."

"Did you know that the Factor's down stairs?"

"No I didn't. What's he doing down there?"

"It's the A.G.M. Of the Rare Sheep Breeder Society"

"Well, that's a bloody laugh. Still, I suppose he's got to go along with it to keep his cover for his other business. Were you speaking to him?" asked Ryan.

"Just for a few minutes, but long enough for him to tell me that, he understood that I had you for company today, and that I wasn't to take you with me anymore, his excuse was that the estate's insurance wouldn't cover you, should you have an accident" explained Stuart.

"I told you that he was well-informed. Still, I suppose he's right enough about the insurance. I am sorry if I have got you into trouble" said Ryan apologetically.

"Don't be, because I'm not." Stuart dismissed Ryan's concern.

"As much as I like being out and about with you Stuart, I don't want to get you into any trouble over me, but I will leave that up to you to decide.

Stuart changed the subject "Are you still intending to go out with Jill the spy on Thursday?"

"I haven't quite decided yet, but I think that I probably will, only in the line of duty you understand?"

"But of course, why would I think any different? Just be careful that she doesn't seduce you."

"Don't worry she won't."

"Okay Ryan I will leave you to it. I am going to have a shower and see if I can get some room service. Give me a call whenever."

"I will do. Good night Stuart"

As Stuart made his way along the corridor to his room, he had a sinking feeling that something bad was around the corner.

35

The next morning Ryan checked out of the hotel, he decided to postpone his date with Jill as it was more important to shake his tail and find a new place to stay. Meantime, he could use Jill to lay a false trail. So, before he started on his journey he left a note at the reception for Jill. It read:

```
Dear Jill as much as I
was looking forward to
our day out,
unfortunately something
has cropped up at work
and I have been summoned
back to London. Perhaps
we can meet another time.
Yours, Ryan Jones.
```

Ryan then started his journey it wasn't long before Ryan picked out the unmarked police car that was following him. He would lose this tail in Glasgow and get a different car there. He had phoned the car hire company, telling them that he wanted to change it for another. He also asked where their nearest depot was. Ryan wasn't very familiar with the layout of Glasgow, but then he thought if he got lost, so might his tail, or at least he would manage to shake them off.

The traffic in Glasgow city centre was quite heavy and slow-moving. As luck would have it, just as he approached a set of traffic lights, they were about to change to red. Ryan kept on going, almost running a red light. Looking in his rear view mirror, he could see that none of the cars had followed him through. "That's sorted you buggers out." said Ryan out loud.

It wasn't long before Ryan found the car-hire garage. Ryan had a back-up plan, should they have seen him go into the garage. He decided to use it just in case. He told the receptionist that he was now staying at the Hilton Hotel in the city centre and asked if they could deliver the car to the hotel for twelve thirty. She said that they would be more than happy to.

Ryan had had a few new ideas over night. Who actually owned the Braes of Brackie Hotel? Ryan intended to find out. He was going to the land registry office to piece together the web of ownership and directorships. He left the hire car office and hailed a taxi to take him back into the city centre.

On the way, as he was looking out of the taxi window, he spotted the unmarked police car that had been following him. They were parked at the side of the road the two men had a rather lost look on their faces. Their boss wasn't going to be very happy with them, thought Ryan.

Ryan found out what he needed to know at the registration office. He then called his boys in London and got the low down on Caledonian Land Holding. It all fitted together rather nicely. The Factor, as Ryan had suspected was a director off Caledonian Land Holdings. Their office was based at the Factor's farm and as he thought it might be, the Braes of Brackie Hotel belonged to Caledonian Land Holdings, and also a catering company, which Ryan suspected was the meat-delivery business. The company had five named directors, two of which were now dead. On his way to the Hilton Hotel, Ryan called his boss in London to pass on the information.

"That's brilliant news Ryan, well done. That's more than enough to justify a warrant. See if you can get access to a computer and write up a report on everything that you know. Try and send it to me as soon as you can and don't do anything else okay? Just sit tight for a day or two. I will start the ball rolling at this end and if all goes well, you should have your back-up in a few days time."

"There's another thing that you should know about."

"What's that Ryan?"

"The Factor has installed a plant at the Braes of Brackie hotel, and a very glamorous one at that but very professional. I was supposed to meet with her on Thursday but I left her a note saying that I couldn't make it. She was definitely up to no good"

"It's a good job that you found this out or you might have found yourself in deep shit. Good work Ryan. I take it that you have moved to a different location and lost your tail?"

"I checked out of the hotel this morning and I've managed to shake off the tail. I am now going to collect a new car and head to another site."

"Good, just keep your head down and your phone handy, because I don't think it will take us long to get the go-ahead"

"Ok Guv I'll be ready and waiting" said Ryan feeling satisfied, the case was drawing to a close.

36

Ryan made sure that he was at the Hilton hotel in time to collect his new car. The next job was to find another place to stay. The guest house that Stuart had suggested sounded ideal, so he decided that he would go and look for it. But the most important thing at the moment was to make sure that he wasn't followed again. After leaving Glasgow, Ryan stopped periodically in lay-bys, making sure that he wasn't being followed. After a while, Ryan was content that he had left his tail back in Glasgow. He continued on his journey with caution.

Ryan drove five maybe six miles past the Braes of Brackie Hotel, staying on the coast road. He had already passed several guest houses but none had the privacy that Ryan was looking for. Just as he was thinking about turning back, Ryan came across a sign for a guest house on the right-hand side of the road. It was the place Stuart had told him about. The driveway to the guest house was at least five hundred yards long, ideal thought Ryan, at least the location was anyway, for it didn't matter what the accommodation was like so long as he was off the main road and out of sight.

To Ryan's surprise, the guest house was very plush. Perfect, thought Ryan. It even had a small business room with a computer and fax machine. Ryan asked at reception and found out that there was only one other person staying there.

The room that Ryan had been allocated was on the second floor, with a large window overlooking the rear car park and gardens. Very pleasant thought Ryan. What more could he ask for? As he gazed out of the window admiring the well kept gardens, he let his mind drift. June, his wife, would have loved it here. This was her ideal type of place; peace and quiet. She would be quite content just to stroll round the gardens, choose a bench to sit at and read her book.

But it wasn't to be. Why was it that she had to die so young? She was such a loving and caring person. She had been the type of person that would do anything for anyone, always putting herself last. Ryan often thought where was the justice in life? Why was it always the innocent that suffered when you have rapists, drug dealers and murderers living a great life, not giving a shit about whose life they ruin? People like the Factor who only care about themselves, greedy for money and a lavish life-style. These thoughts made Ryan angry. He swore to himself that he would get the Factor and put an end to his little empire, unless of course Hodges got to the Factor first.

Ryan gazed out into the gardens for a long time, going over in his mind everything that had happened up to now. It all started with the murders in London, murders committed by a professional killer. A professional killer who has started his own one-man crusade seeking revenge for the death of his cousin, the crusade had now taken him north of the border to Scotland where he continues with his personal vendetta.

Hodges was maybe doing the country a big favour by ridding it of drug dealers, but Ryan knew he had to stop him somehow. Personal vendetta or not, Russell Hodges was a murderer, maybe so to was Stuart Brodie, Ryan suspected more went on in Asia than Stuart is admitting to. "But Asia is not my patch where as London and the UK is, so it is up to me to stop Hodges and if I need Stuart's help then I will have to take it" reasoned Ryan.

But Stuart Brodie, what is he? Friend or foe? Ryan still wasn't completely convinced of Stuart's innocence in these UK murders. Maybe he was still in cahoots with Russell Hodges? Feeding him information perhaps? Stuart did however, seem quite concerned about the mysterious Dr. Russell, but there again, that could quite easily be a ploy as well.

Ryan wasn't quite sure what to think anymore. It was as if half a dozen cases were rolled into one, but they all had one thing in common; everyone it seems, has links with the estate one way or another. The estate was owned by Jason Bellingham, who up until five years ago was the most corrupt and dangerous man in Britain, a man that had desperately wanted D.S Ryan Jones dead and if it hadn't been for Rachael, Jason's wife, he would have succeeded.

Was the Factor aware of the criminal past of the present owner of the estate? The Factor could be working for Bellingham in more ways than one, Factoring his and managing his drugs ring or is the Factor operating on his own, the main man of the largest drug organization in the U.K.? Either way, he is about to be shut down.

Ryan decided after a great deal of thought and deliberation, that the only thing that he could do was to go with the flow once the Factor was in custody more evidence would come to light. He just hoped there would be no more deaths. He knew if the Bellingham's were involved he could very well be in danger, not that he was afraid of dying. There was once a contract out on his life, at that time Ryan had kind of gotten used to the idea that all life was expendable, even his own.

Ryan wasn't a religious man, although he had prayed to God when his wife June was dying. The thought of being with her again some day, eased the thought of his own death.

Or maybe it was his guilty conscience? He had carried that guilt with him for over twelve years; it was his own skeleton in the closet. Ryan was hoping that the Bellingham's were oblivious as to what was going on at their Scottish highland estate. For Ryan didn't relish the thought of encountering them ever again.

37

Jason Bellingham was a control freak and also a very manipulative and evil person. He was into everything from drugs, extortion, prostitution to reset and woe be-tide anyone that crossed him or didn't pay up. Not only would he send round his heavies to sort them out, but he would go along with them to make sure that the punishment was severe enough.

The prostitutes that worked for Jason all hated him; he would make them have sordid sex with his heavies. If they didn't comply, they were beaten up and thrown out onto the streets. He told them that he wanted to make sure that the punters were getting good value for their money, but the prostitutes reckoned it was for his own sick pleasure, because he used to like to watch and would shout at them if they didn't make the appropriate noises at the right time. Any lubricating gel that needed applying, he would do himself, ramming his fingers home hard.

It was a prostitute called Mandy that brought about the investigation into the affairs of Jason and Rachael Bellingham. Mandy was one of the few prostitutes that didn't comply with the sexual demands made by Jason Bellingham. She was found in the street so badly-beaten that she almost died. It had taken almost three weeks before Ryan was able to question her. Even then, Mandy had great difficulty in speaking, as her jaw had been broken in three different places. Her other injuries consisted of a fractured skull, a broken collar-bone and three broken ribs, plus severe bruising. Mandy told Ryan everything that went on at 'Scandals', the name of the night club that the Bellingham's owned. There was an illegal gambling room at the back, as well as two rooms where the prostitutes worked. There were a further three rooms upstairs; one was an office, the other two, the girls used for entertaining the clients.

Ryan first visited Scandals night club under cover. He wanted to get a feel for the place before he started investigating. He was very surprised at the fact that everything was quite open, even the gambling room, as long as you had at least five hundred pounds to spend. The prostitutes mingled with the guests at the bars. There were three bars altogether, two in the dance area and a cocktail lounge. One of the prostitutes had approached Ryan on the first night. He had contemplated going with her, but decided against it. He would keep his interviewing to daytime hours as the prostitutes would be more likely to talk when they weren't working.

Ryan didn't go back to Scandals night club until three days later. He spent those three days finding out as much as possible about the Bellingham's. Just as Ryan had expected, Jason Bellingham had his fingers in a lot pies, but he only had one company registered in his name. That company was a second-hand car dealer's garage, which specialised in prestigious cars. Scandals night club was owned by his wife Rachael, or was at least under her name. She also owned two rather upmarket beauty parlours. It was at one these that Ryan was to first encounter Rachael.

Over that three-day period, Ryan had liaised with the drug squad, the vice squad and the fraud squad. Between them they had gathered enough information related to the Bellingham's most of which concerned illegal businesses. Warrants were issued and several raids and arrests took place. Seven businesses were shut down and a total of thirty-three people were arrested, including Jason Bellingham.

On the day of Bellingham's arrest Ryan had arrived at Scandals night club at nine o'clock in the morning. With him were another two detectives and four uniformed officers. They had with them the appropriate warrants; one for the search of the premises and three for arrests. As luck would have it, the side door to the building was open. Two of the uniformed officers remained at the door. Ryan thought that if anyone was going to make a run for it, it would be out through the side door.

Ryan had a good idea of the layout inside the night club from his previous visit and also from what Mandy had told him. They had no sooner entered the building when they stopped, turned and looked at one another. The door to the games room at the back was open and coming from it was a continuous groaning sound. The sound was not of the pleasurable kind, it was a pitiful, painful wailing. Ryan made his way over to the door, followed by his colleagues, not sure what to expect. Ryan slowly put his head around the edge of the door. What he saw before him made him cringe.

"Stop what you're doing right now." shouted Ryan in a very angry voice.

"Jesus Christ." said one of Ryan's colleagues at the sight.

The scene that they witnessed was like something out of a porn film. Side on to them bent over a table in the centre of the room was a young girl. Her arms were outstretched Jason Bellingham held by her wrists pulling her forward. The girl's feet were off the ground and hard behind her was one of Bellingham's heavies. He was thrusting himself into her so hard that the table, on every thrust, lifted off the ground. This was obviously giving him pleasure by the expression on his face, but for the girl, by the groans that she was letting out, it sounded more like torture. To the far side of the table stood one of Bellingham's other henchmen who held in his hand his erect penis.

"What the fuck are you doing in here?" growled Jason Bellingham, as he let go of the girl's wrists. At the same time, the heavy known as 'Clubs' withdrew himself from the girl and the other heavy quickly pulled up his trousers. The girl slumped to the floor and curled up into a foetal position. Blood trickled down the side of her left buttock. It seemed to be coming from her rectum.

"Will someone cover up that poor girl and you better call an ambulance."

Ryan took several pieces of paper from his pocket and held them up.

"What I have here, is warrants for your arrests and one to search the premises."

"What do you mean arrests? We haven't done anything wrong."

"You are under arrest for the attempted murder of Mandy Williams, illegal gambling, drug dealing, fraud and what we have just witnessed, gang rape."

"Who the fuck are you?"

"D.S. Jones. Now put your hands behind your back"

"You're a dead man Jones."

"That's another charge; threatening a police officer, now cuff him."

"I want to make a phone call." growled Bellingham.

"You can make your phone call at the station."

The uniformed officers escorted Jason Bellingham and his two henchmen through the night club and out the side door. Ryan went over to the girl who was now sitting on a seat, bent double. A towel draped over her slim shoulders. She clutched this tightly around her middle.

"What's your name love?" asked Ryan in a caring voice.

"Kirsty." said the girl, and then burst into a flood of tears.

Ryan sat in the chair next to her and put his arm around her "Its okay love, no one's going to abuse and hurt you anymore" Ryan reassured her.

Ryan felt a lump in his throat and tears build up in his eyes at the thought of what this poor girl had just been put through. She was probably younger than his own daughter.

"Do you work here Kirsty?"

"Yes, I started here three days ago."

"Do you know if there are any other girls in the building?"

"I don't think so. I was told last night to come in this morning for training."

"Listen, don't worry about this. Everything will be fine. There's an ambulance on the way. A W.P.C will come and see you at the hospital, okay?"

"You won't tell my parents about this will you?"

"No Kirsty, we won't. That is entirely up to you." Ryan sat with his arm around the girl until the ambulance arrived. He thought to himself, Bellingham you bastard; I will see that you swing for this.

38

Ryan and the other two detectives did a random search of the building. In the office upstairs they found a considerable amount of cash, along with what seemed to be about half a kilo of cocaine. One of the detectives clicked on the office computer.

"Have a look at this boss."

Ryan and his other colleague went over to have a look.

"The fucking pervert, only a sick bastard would look at this sort of stuff. Right, unplug it. We'll take it with us. Jason Bellingham, you are going to jail for a long time."

"He seemed pretty mad at you boss."

"Who wouldn't be, if they were caught in the act doing what he was doing?"

"That poor girl, she looked terrified"

"She was. Some training session and if she resisted she would have ended up like Mandy Williams"

"What a bastard he is. I would like to be left alone in a room with him for ten minutes." said the detective clenching his fists.

"Yes, wouldn't we all? Okay you two, get this stuff down to the station. I am going to pay Mrs Bellingham a visit."

Ryan parked his car opposite the beauty parlour. The shop-front looked very plush and up-market. The sign above the door read 'Rachael's Beauty Salon'. Ryan wondered to himself what type of woman Rachael Bellingham would be. Would she be anything like her perverted husband? Only one way to find out thought Ryan, as he got out of the car and headed over to the salon.

The minute Ryan walked through the door of the salon; the pleasant aromatic smell filled his nostrils. Inside was so plush that Ryan felt that he had just entered the foyer to a grand hotel. Everything about it was pure luxury. Seated on one of the rather expensive-looking settees were two rather glamorous young ladies and another was seated behind a glass desk. Ryan wondered if the two beauties seated on the couch were clients or staff. All three of them looked and smiled at Ryan as he entered. The young lady pushed back her seat and rose to her feet, the see-through desk unable to hide how scantily dressed she was.

"Good morning Sir, do you have an appointment?"

"No I don't, unfortunately."

"Would you like to make one Sir?"

"No thanks, well not at the moment anyway. I was actually hoping to see Mrs Bellingham. Is she here?"

"Yes she is, but she's having a facial at the moment. If you'd like to take a seat, I will tell her that you are here. Can I have your name Sir?"

"Yes, it's Detective Sergeant Ryan Jones."

There was a sudden change of expression on the young ladies face. Ryan glanced at the two beauties sitting on the couch. Their expressions had also changed, as they glanced at each other. Ryan's assumption of what went on here behind the scenes was correct. The two beauties were in fact members of staff. The young receptionist returned after being gone for five minutes. Probably being debriefed on what not to say, thought Ryan.

"Mrs Bellingham will be with you as soon as she can Mr Jones. Can I get you a coffee or a soft drink perhaps?"

"A coffee would be nice thanks."

"What do you take in your coffee Sir?"

"Just black thanks."

Ryan sat on a velvet sofa opposite the two beauties and gave them a smile, which they promptly returned. Ryan had an inward laugh to himself, at the shock that he gave them when he told them who was.

The lady that walked towards Ryan made him raise his eyebrows. She looked absolutely stunning. Ryan rose to his feet.

"Hello, I am Rachael Bellingham."

"Hello, D.S. Jones." said Ryan accepting her out-stretched hand.

"How can I help you Detective?"

"Is there somewhere private that we can talk?"

"Yes, I have an office through the back."

Ryan followed her, admiring her figure as she walked, her perfume over-powering the already scented room. She stopped at the see-through desk.

"Kitty, will you make sure that we are not disturbed"

"Yes, Mrs Bellingham."

Her office was as luxurious as the reception area, maybe even more so with a cocktail bar giving the room a decadent air.

"Please have seat Detective. Can I get you a drink?" her voice was cultured with no trace of an accent.

"No thanks, Mrs Bellingham."

"Please call me Rachael. Now tell me what is this all about"

"We arrested your husband this morning." Ryan watched her closely for a reaction. There wasn't any.

"What for, may I ask?"

"The attempted murder of Mandy Williams" Ryan explained

"Who is she?" inquired Rachael.

"A girl that used to work at Scandals, your night club."

"I don't know the girl; in fact I don't know anyone who works there."

"But it is your night club, is it not"

"Only on paper I have never even set foot in the place."

"So you've no idea what goes on there?"

"None whatsoever and I don't even want to know. My husband and I lead very different lives."

"That maybe so Mrs Bellingham, sorry Rachael, but I think that you both run similar businesses."

"What do you mean similar businesses? I happen to run two very successful beauty salons."

"Come on Rachael, I wasn't born yesterday. They are maybe high-class, but I can spot a prostitute when I see one."

"So tell me what happened to this girl Mandy?" Ryan could tell by the change in her tone and of subject that he had hit the nail right on the head.

"Does your husband ever come here Rachael?"

"No, he doesn't. What happened to the girl?"

"Why doesn't he come here?"

"Like I said earlier Detective, we have our separate lives."

"I think that the reason Jason doesn't come here is because you won't allow him to, am I correct?"

"That's right, but so what?"

"So you know what type of man your husband is then?"

"I should do, I have been married to him for nine years. Are you going to tell me what happened or not?"

"Mandy Williams worked for your husband, but she wouldn't comply with his perverse sexual tendencies so he had her beaten up and thrown out onto the street, so badly that she almost died."

"But Jason wouldn't beat anyone up."

"That's maybe so, but he instigates it and he likes to watch." Rachael sat quietly in her chair with her head lowered in shame. The truth about her husband obviously hurt.

"When Jason and I were first married, he was such a lovely person. We would do everything together. We even had great sex. Then, for some reason, after about four years, he suddenly became impotent. Even the doctors couldn't explain why. They tried all sorts of tests and drugs, but nothing worked and he changed completely. He became a monster, frustrated and very aggressive."

"Did he ever abuse or beat you up Rachael?"

"No never, whenever he got angry he would take off somewhere for a few days. Where he went, or what he got up to, I have no idea. All I know is that when he came back, he was back to his caring and loving self and that's the way it still is."

"How can you live with him knowing that he's such a brutal and violent man?"

"Maybe it's because of what we once had together, or maybe its pity or both. I don't really know"

"What do you know about your husband's other activities, other than the night club Rachael?"

"All I know about is the second-hand car business that he has. Other than that I don't know what else he does."

"Well, apart from being charged with attempted murder, he is also charged with illegal gambling, fraud and drug dealing, not to mention what we witnessed this morning when we arrested him. Your husband will be going to jail for some time Rachael."

Rachael was now beginning to sob; Ryan for some reason felt sorry for her and thought it was time to back off for a while.

"Listen Rachael, I am going to leave you in peace for a while, but I will need to speak with you again okay?"

"Yes okay, but you don't have to come back here do you?"

"No, we can meet wherever you like. I will give you a call."

"Thanks."

Ryan left the so-called beauty salon. On the way out, he noticed that the two beauties had gone. Sitting on the sofa in their place was a rather smartly-dressed young businessman"

"In for a facial are you?" asked Ryan sarcastically.

"No a manicure actually" he replied

"Of course you are." Ryan shook his head and walked outside.

He wondered if Rachael was on the game herself and perhaps this gentleman was one of her clients. If so, he doubted whether she would be very passionate today.

39

It took three months before Jason Bellingham was sentenced. The attempted murder charge was reduced to grievous bodily harm. He was also sentenced for fraud, extortion, illegal gambling and prostitution. He got a total of five years in jail, but he would only serve three of them. His henchmen and cronies all got prison sentences ranging from three years to five years. During the three-month trial period, it came to light through various sources, that there was a contract out on Ryan's life.

Ryan had met with Rachael Bellingham on another two occasions to discuss her involvement with the Scandals night club and her own beauty salons. Ryan was convinced however, that she knew nothing at all about what went on at the night club. As for her own beauty salons, Ryan didn't see any point in pursuing the fact that she offered services other than beauty treatments.

Ryan became quite concerned about the contract that was out on him, as were his colleagues at work. There had been several anonymous phone calls to the police station, stating that he was 'a walking dead man'. Although these threats scared Ryan, his main concern had been for his wife June. She was now seriously ill in hospital and Ryan knew that she didn't have long to live. One day, out of the blue, Ryan got a phone call from Rachael Bellingham. She wanted to meet with him at her house. Rightly or wrongly, Ryan went to meet her. The driveway to the house was lit up but at the same time, the house was secluded from the main road which alleviated Ryan's fear of being spotted at her house. The front door of the house opened before Ryan got out of the car. Rachael stood in the doorway looking as stunning as ever.

"Hello Rachael, how are you?"

"Good evening Detective. I am very well thank-you. Please come in."

Ryan entered the house. It was as lavish as he had expected it to be.

"Can I get you a drink Detective?"

"No thanks and you can call me Ryan, especially now that the investigation has finished."

"Okay Ryan, please take a seat."

Ryan sat down on one of the cream-coloured leather chairs. He felt like he was going to sink in it all the way to the floor.

"So why do you want to see me Rachael? Is there something that I can do for you?"

"No Ryan, well not exactly, it's more what I can do for you, or should I say what I have done for you."

"What do you mean Rachael, done for me?"

"I have had the contract on your life stopped."

"You know about that, how?" Ryan couldn't take it in.

"Well I am still married to the man who put out the contract"

"How did you manage to talk him out of it, and why?" said Ryan amazed and grateful.

"I simply told him that if he didn't stop the contract, then I wouldn't be here when he gets out of jail. Why? Well you always treated me with respect and I am sure if you had wanted to, you could have closed down my salons."

"Maybe I will have that drink after all." said Ryan, for he now felt as if a great burden had been lifted from his shoulders.

It wasn't until the small hours of the morning, that Ryan realised he had missed the message on his pager. By the time he reached the hospital, he was too late, June had slipped away. Ryan sat holding her hand and wept for over an hour. The feeling of guilt would live with him for the rest of his life.

40

That Wednesday morning Stuart had woken earlier than usual, for he'd had a restless night. He had kept thinking about Sharon during the night, wondering if they would have got more serious, or just stayed friends and occasional lovers. Stuart preferred the latter thought, as he suspected that he would never get into a serious relationship again. He did however feel sad that she had been killed, especially for her two young children. Or maybe it was more a feeling of anger that he felt. All he knew was that whoever killed Sharon deserved to die and by the look of things, they had. As to who was responsible for their deaths, one person came to Stuart's mind.

Stuart washed, got dressed and made his way down to the gun room. Stuart had decided to give the big wood a miss today. He felt that he'd seen enough ghosts in the wood for the time being. He wished brought his Manlicher .270 rifle from home, as that was his favoured rifle for the open hill.

The rifle that Stuart had brought was his .308, which was best-suited for woodland stalking. It was just as lethal as a .270, but it had a slower bullet that did not break up so easy if it came into contact with a twig or even a clump of bracken, unlike the .270, a faster bullet, which could deflect or break up, even by touching a blade of grass.

The .270 was however the best rifle for the open hill, because of its faster bullet. The .270 also had a straighter trajectory and more of a clout which in turn meant that when it struck its target, if it was of the living kind, death was instant. Even with a bad shot, the quarry was not going far whether it is a leg or haunch, for once struck with the shear force and velocity of the bullet, that part of the body was disabled completely.

Stuart had been witness to a lot of poor marksmen over the years, some so bad that they should never been allowed to use firearms in the first place. Albeit their target shooting might be very accurate, but when it came to shooting a large stag or hind even, they simply fell to bits. Most suffered what is known as 'buck fever', a symptom caused by nerves, or too big an adrenalin rush. They would shake profusely making it impossible for an accurate and clean shot.

Others were just too impatient. The thought of their prize, or trophy running off was just too much for them to bear. A hastily-taken shot usually ended up with the beast running off anyway, to die a slow and painful death. More often than not, such casualties were most likely to have been shot in the gut.

In some countries it is illegal to hunt game without a trained tracking dog for such incidents, should they occur. In the U.K. however, it is not compulsory yet, but many professional deer stalkers do have them especially the stalkers that take out clients. Most of the gun-dog breeds can be trained to track wounded deer, the most popular being Labradors, or Tekkels, which are a German breed from the Dachshund family. Others such as spaniels, are inclined to be distracted by the scent of other animals, leading their handlers on a wild goose chase and often end up losing the wounded beast altogether.

Stuart had a Tekkel himself for a number of years, but he gave the dog to a keen young deer stalker before he moved abroad. The dog, as far as Stuart knew, was well looked-after and still going strong to this day. After being away for four years, Stuart didn't have the heart to ask for the dog back.

Outside the back of the hotel, Stuart stopped as he always did and took in a deep breath of the cool early morning air. Stuart knew how great it was to have freedom, for this was what life was all about; being able to get up in the morning and walking out into the fresh air, knowing that no-one had any hold over you whatsoever.

When Stuart went to his Land Rover he noticed the two policemen sleeping in their unmarked car. It was the same two that had been given the detail of following Ryan, but Stuart knew that Ryan would soon give them the slip, if he hadn't already.

Stuart headed for West Crag. It was going to be a nice day and he could not think of a better place to be. By the time Stuart arrived at the Crag, the sun was shining through the light cloud indicating a warm day ahead. Stuart parked the Land Rover in the usual spot. After sitting for several minutes, he got his things together. He crept forward to the edge of the Crag with the same care as usual. Not knowing what to expect once he got there, for every day was different.

Gazing over the area before him, Stuart noticed the large group of deer out on the basin. He counted twenty-seven, mainly hinds with several calves and three young stags. The young stags were a sure sign that the rut was not far away. Being over-eager to sow their seeds, occasionally, a few hinds would come into season early. Their scent would drift in the wind for miles, enticing the stags down from the higher ground.

The mature stags of the hierarchy would bide their time and save their energy for fighting off rivals, the victors gaining domination over the hinds, which succumbed more readily to the mature stags advances.

The young stags were soon put in their place, pushed to the side to become spectators. Their turn would come, but not this year or for many others, not until they become strong enough to challenge the mature stags to a battle which often resulted in serious injury or even death.

Survival of the fittest that was for sure and the hinds realised this for they would only stand for these strong, mature stags, ensuring that they would produce a good, healthy calf the following year. But the sad thing about it all, is that none of these red deer, or at least very few of them would be participating in this year's rut or any other. For their death warrant had already been signed.

Stuart often wondered whether there was a physical attraction between deer, or was it just the fact that the hinds were bullied into submission? Maybe it was a bit of both, or natural instinct, not unlike human behaviour really. As for the deer on this hill, there would be no survivors. In a way you could say that they were on death row. Only the deer were oblivious to the fact as they sat lazily chewing their cud, enjoying the moment.

Stuart cast his gaze along the ridges that surrounded the basin, homing in on any shapes and colours that were not part of the landscape. On the ridge to the left of the basin, Stuart spotted a fox stealthily making its way towards the cairn where they have their cubs every year. Probably the same fox that he saw a few mornings ago. Turning his attention to the opposite side of the basin, to Stuart's surprise high up on a rocky ridge there were two large stags. They were basking in the morning sun, storing their energy for the forth-coming rut that lay ahead. At the moment it looks like they are the best of friends just now, thought

Stuart, but in a few weeks time they will become mortal enemies and fight each other for supremacy over the hinds.

As Stuart was contemplating whether to go for the two large stags, a Golden Eagle glided into view no more than a few hundred yards from where Stuart sat. The eagle veered towards Stuart, obviously wanting to have a closer look at him. Perhaps thinking that he might be a possible meal, or maybe just curious at the sight of a different colour and shape. They were, after all, both predators in their own way. Satisfied with the survey, the eagle effortlessly soared above Stuart and was gone.

Stuart felt a great sense of privilege at seeing the eagle so close in it's natural habitat, for he knew that some people had never seen one, other than on the television or at a zoo. In Stuart's mind, to cage these magnificent birds was criminal, even if they were captive-bred.

Stuart thought back to when he was a captive behind bars in Asia, albeit for a few days only. It was pure hell and the conditions were atrocious. Crammed in a cage with thirty other people was anything but pleasant. They were the type that would set upon you and rob you of whatever belongings you had, even your shoes. Sleep was totally out of the question for you might not wake up. The filth and stench was disgusting. There were no toilets or privacy whatsoever. All that was available to relieve yourself in were buckets which were emptied once a day. The animals in a zoo were better cared for, but then they probably deserved better. When he was released, Stuart swore to himself that he would never be in that position again, he would rather die first.

41

Two hours later, after a long hike, working his way up and down corries, Stuart found himself in an awkward position, for all he could see of the stags were their large antlers sticking up from behind the rocks. Stuart tried his approach at different angles, but it was the same either way. Only one thing for it, thought Stuart, he would have to get the stags to stand, as it could take hours for them to stand on their own.

Stuart made his way carefully to what he thought would be a good vantage point above the stags. The back-drop was good, only open space leading to the basin below. It was safe to shoot, unless someone on extremely tall stilts walked by.

He picked up a small rock and flung it to the right of where the stags lay. Mounting the rifle to his shoulder, he waited for them to stand up. Nothing happened. All that he could see were their large antlers turning towards the direction of where the rock had landed. Stuart threw another rock and this time they rose quickly to their feet. Being less than forty yards away, the stags looked like giants through the scope on the rifle. Without hesitation, Stuart shot the first stag in the side of the neck. The second one turned its head in surprise and took the next bullet just below the left ear. Stuart re-loaded the rifle and waited for any sign of movement but all was still and quiet.

Stuart began to make his way forward to where the two dead stags lay. He had only gone a few yards when suddenly he froze. Stuart heard stones clattering down the hillside from behind. Instinctively he crouched to the ground before turning around. It was a sound that he was familiar with, a sound caused by deer clambering up or along the side of a rocky hill and in their haste, loosening some of the smaller rocks.

Stuart slid over to a large rock, seeing it as a potential rifle rest, for the two stags that were making their way up the hill were now the new targets. The stags were about one hundred and fifty yards away and still moving. Stuart prepared for a shot for he knew that the stags could stop at any time, like most animals do when they are not sure of what has caused them to flee in the first place. Sure enough, the two stags stopped and looked back down the hill.

Stuart deliberately shot the lead stag first, hoping to prevent the other one from taking off up the hill any further. The plan worked; the second stag was now making its way back down the hill, but he didn't get very far. Both dead stags tumbled and rolled down the hill, their sheer body-weight driving them forward. More and more rocks became dislodged and rumbled down the rocky hillside before coming to rest sixty or seventy yards below. Within a few minutes, all was quiet again.

The last two stags which Stuart had shot, came to rest along with fallen rocks on a flat area of the hillside, as luck would have it, for this was the very spot Stuart had intended to drag the first two stags he had shot. Steve would be able to reach the spot with the Argocat with ease.

After gralloching and dragging the beasts together, Stuart sat down and cast his eye over the landscape. Not that he was expecting to see much, for during all the commotion the other deer in the area would now be long gone.

The only thing that caught Stuart's eye was the flash of light, high up on the hill at the far end of the basin. There it was again, Stuart was sure of what it was this time. It was caused by the sun reflecting on glass; someone was spying on him.

It was one of those times Stuart was glad he had his binoculars with him. He picked out the spy easily enough but due to the glare of the reflection from the sun on the person's binoculars now magnified by his own, Stuart was unable to make out who the person was.

He put down his binoculars and waited until the other person did the same. As soon as the light was gone, Stuart raised his binoculars just in time to see a figure slip over the horizon. The person that had been spying on Stuart obviously didn't want to be recognised but Stuart knew who it was by the speed and agility that got them over the top of the hill so quickly.

What was Russell doing out on the hill? He was not just out for an afternoon stroll, thought Stuart. No, he was following him, but why? What was his motive? It had been the same at the quarry yesterday morning and in the big wood, Russell was stalking him. At the same time, Russell was making sure that Stuart always got a glimpse of him, Why?

Was this his way of trying to unnerve Stuart before a showdown? If it was, then it was certainly working for Stuart felt very uneasy.

Only time would tell what the outcome would be, in the meantime, all Stuart could do was wait and hope that he wasn't on Russell's hit list. For Stuart was worried about just how pissed-off Russell might be about Stuart running out on him.

42

Stuart thought back to some of the good times he and Russell had shared together in Asia. One such time, they went on a safari, not by vehicle but on elephants. That was quite an experience in itself, sitting on top of one the most majestic animals in the world, sauntering along at a lazy pace, having plenty of time to take in the breathtaking sights and scenes of dark green hills, palm trees, lush vegetation and bright parrot-like birds.

There were five of us on that particular trek, mused Stuart thinking back, myself, Russell and three men from Europe. We had two guides, one on the lead elephant and one on the rear. All of the elephants were attached to each other, not with ropes or chains, but by their trunks and tails for each one held onto the one in front and if the lead elephant stopped, then we all stopped. We had no control over the mighty beasts whatsoever; we just sat there as mighty men.

The trek was lasted five days with stops each day at a different camp site. The camp-sites consisted of reasonably-sized huts constructed of bamboo with thatched roofs. Inside each hut was a three-quarter sized wooden bed with a thin mattress and pillows on top. The beds were shrouded with mosquito nets, as was the door. Behind each of the huts there were smaller huts which contained a chemical toilet and a large wash tub that could accommodate two people. The camps themselves and their facilities were a bit primitive, but considering that the camps were situated in the back-of-beyond, in almost jungle surroundings, they were in reality very comfortable and welcoming, especially after sitting astride an elephant for six hours at a time, in such a humid climate with the sun blazing down on you.

Unfortunately, elephants in their natural environment do smell quite a bit, unlike the ones at the zoo. So after a long, hot, sticky day riding one, the camps were a welcome sight, especially the bath tubs. On arrival at the camps, each person was allocated a personal aide. These aides were in the form of beautiful young ladies. They tended to our every need, starting with a thorough wash in the tub and a massage.

The evening at the first camp-site would always be the most memorable, in more ways than one. After eating an excellent meal and having a few drinks, Russell and I retired to our huts with our escorts. This however, was short-lived, for the three Europeans in our group had managed to get drunk and become very aggressive to our hosts for some reason.

When Russell and I tried to calm the situation they simply turned on us, which was a big mistake on their part. Within seconds, all three were lying unconscious on the ground, with blood oozing from their noses and mouths. Russell had dropped two of them like flies with a couple of well judged blows. I blocked the other's attempt and head-butted him square in the face, on his way to the ground, I brought my knee up under his chin, which sent him sprawling backwards. We helped carry them into their huts where they remained peacefully for the rest of the night.

In the morning they were very apologetic to everyone, even the man whose nose I had broken. For the rest of the trek they were very humble, in fact they were the first to retire each evening with their escorts.

Putting Russell out of his thoughts for the time being Stuart started making his way back along the hillside. He remembered that he forgot to tell Steve that he wanted him at hand today, but Stuart knew that as soon as Steve got the phone-call he would drop whatever he was doing and head straight out.

Steve was always looking for an excuse to get away from his mundane chores, especially if those chores involved sheep.

Back at the Land Rover, Stuart called Steve and told him where the beasts were lying. He then called Ryan. They chatted briefly and arranged to meet early the next morning. Stuart would go and pick him up at his new lodgings. Ryan had decided against going out with Jill. He told Stuart that he had gained all the information that was required to set the wheels in motion. He was just waiting on word from his boss, to arrest the Factor and raid his farm.

43

Ryan hadn't mentioned anything to Stuart about the Bellingham's, for no-one knew for sure if their involvement on the estate was anything other than being the owners. Ryan hoped that this would be the case, because he didn't want another run-in with either of them. Even just thinking back, to what was a long time ago brought back such bad memories he hoped his past would stay buried.

Ryan spent most of the day in the business room at his new lodgings, typing up his report. He prayed that word of the raid would come sooner than later, before Russell Hodges struck again.

After e-mailing the report to his chief he returned to his room, Ryan was pondering things over when he glanced out of the window. His gaze drifted over the gardens when his attention was caught by a car coming up the drive into the car park. It was a dark blue people carrier with tinted windows. This must be the other guest though Ryan. The person who got out of the car was about five feet ten inches tall and of medium build. He was wearing a dark grey suit, black shirt, with no tie.

Ryan's eye was caught by his choice of footwear. The shoes looked like some type of leather slippers, hardly the things to wear with a suit thought Ryan. But then again, a lot of people find it more comfortable to wear something casual when they are driving. The other thing Ryan noticed about the driver was how well-tanned he was, it wasn't the type of tan that you pick up on your annual holiday. This man had a very deep, well-established tan that you only get by spending a lot of time in hot countries. Maybe he was foreign, that could explain it, thought Ryan. The driver took a hold-all from the car and made his way towards the back entrance of the guest house. As he did so, he glanced up at Ryan. Their eyes met for a few seconds.

Ryan decided that he would go for a stroll around the gardens. As he stepped out of his room, he very nearly bumped into the man he had seen in the car park.

"I am very sorry." said Ryan, taken by surprise.

"That's okay, I wasn't paying attention myself. By the way, my name is John Farrell." the man said, putting his hand out.

"Hi, pleased to meet you. I am Ryan Jones. Have you just finished work?"

"Yes, it's been quite a long day and I am in dire need of a shower" replied the man.

"Just going for a stroll myself perhaps I will see you at dinner?"

"I am sure you will, for I think we are the only two staying here."

"Okay, I will see you later then." said Ryan and he set off along the corridor, thinking to himself that John Farrell seemed a pleasant sort and it might be quite nice to having some company over dinner.

Out in the garden, Ryan thought over his brief encounter, John was definitely British, although he couldn't place the accent. He seemed a nice enough chap, very well-mannered and had a very firm handshake. Judging by his dress and his confident easy manner, Ryan guessed he was a sales person. He would find out more about him at dinner the detective in Ryan, was curious.

Ryan felt sad and melancholy wandering through the garden. He missed June and this was the type of place she would have loved. They would have strolled through the gardens hand in hand admiring the flowers and shrubs. June had been a very keen gardener and could name almost every plant that she came across by its Latin name. Ryan often said a prayer for her, hoping that she was in a beautiful garden somewhere, waiting for him.

The guest house was situated on a hillside with gardens stretching behind the house up the hill, Ryan sat on a bench near the top of the garden and was able to look over the tree tops and out towards the sea he had a spectacular view of the rugged deep gray mountains on the distant islands. The shapes and colours as the clouds swept over them. Ryan was quite inspired at the sight. If only he could paint, he thought to himself. Unfortunately for Ryan, painting was a talent that he didn't possess. He did however appreciate good art so maybe he could learn to paint someday perhaps when he retired from the police force thought Ryan he should take up a hobby. Ryan reluctantly got up from the bench and made his way back towards the guest house.

Back in his room, Ryan changed his clothes for dinner. He was feeling quite hungry after his walk around the gardens. He was also looking forward to having a chat with John Farrell.

When Ryan arrived in the dining room, John Farrell was already seated at a table close to one of the bay windows. This table was set for two. The dining room itself was slightly larger than an average house sitting room. There were six tables, evenly-spaced, with four chairs at each. It was quite a pleasant room with a nice warm feel to it. The floor was covered with a thick pink deep-pile carpet. The bottom half of the walls was painted terracotta and above the dado rail there was cream wallpaper with a small floral print. On the walls hung several oil paintings with gilded frames, all of paintings were of seascapes. The large bay window was draped in long curtains made of Black Watch tartan cloth. Yes, very nice indeed, thought Ryan, as he sat down at the place set opposite John Farrell.

"Did you enjoy your walk?" asked John.

"Yes I did thanks. It's good to stretch the legs and get a breath of fresh air before dinner."

"I quite agree, but after driving for most of the day, a shower was more needed."

"What is it that you work at John, if you don't mind me asking?"

"No not at all. I work for different companies selling life insurance. I travel up and down the country and on the continent."

"Well, you've certainly picked up a good tan on your travels" observed Ryan.

"And what about yourself, what line of work are you in Ryan?"

"I am a civil servant. I have a few days holiday and I thought it would be nice to get away from London for a break, somewhere peaceful and quiet. I haven't seen much of Scotland in the past, so I thought I would take the opportunity to do a bit of touring, stopping here and there."

"Good evening gentlemen. I hope you don't mind eating together?" asked Mrs Campbell, the owner of the guest house, as she approached their table.

"Not at all" said Ryan and John simultaneously.

"In fact it's nice to have some company." said Ryan.

"That's good. Seeing as you are the only two staying here at the moment, I thought I would sit you together. It helps to keep a happy atmosphere. Now what would you like to eat gentlemen? It's scotch broth or leak and potato soup, followed by venison stew or haggis, neaps and tatties, with apple pie and cream for desert."

John opted for the Scotch broth and the haggis. Ryan decided to have the same soup followed by the venison stew. Both of them wanted the apple pie with cream.

"And what would you like to drink?"

"I would like a bottle of lager please." said Ryan.

"And for yourself Mr Farrell what would you like to drink?" asked Mrs Campbell.

"Can I have a large glass of fresh orange please?"

"Certainly." replied Mrs Campbell. She turned away from the table and headed towards the kitchen as quietly as she had come.

Ryan and John made small-talk about the guest house and the area until Mrs Campbell returned with their drinks.

"You don't drink alcohol John?"

"No I don't. I have become tee-total over the years, with the amount of driving that I do, I like to wake up in the morning with a clear head."

"I have to agree with you on that one. Unfortunately, I like to have a few beers when I am not working" said Ryan ruefully.

"That's common practise in the police force I believe."

"Yes, I suppose you're right. It's a way of relieving the stress of the job." said Ryan, taken slightly aback by the directness of John's remark.

"And what about you John? Have you always worked in insurance?"

"No I used to work on the oil rigs for quite a lot of years."

"Here's your soup gentlemen. Now mind it's hot" instructed Mrs Campbell who appeared at the table as quietly as before and left again with a swish of her long skirt.

"Are you married Ryan?" probed John Farrell.

"My wife died about five years ago and my daughter lives in Canada with her husband. She's expecting her first child. What about you?"

"Never been married and I don't expect I ever will. I enjoy my freedom too much. Its good being able to come and go as you please, when and where you want."

The conversation dwindled during the rest of the meal. John Farrell seemed to fit the sales person type very well, thought Ryan he had that over confident and arrogant air that often made a good sales person. Ryan wasn't sure whether he liked Farrell or not and he sensed the feeling was mutual and Farrell wasn't sure whether he liked Ryan. Still, it had at least been a bit of company during dinner.

44

The next morning Stuart woke up early as usual, had a shower, got dressed in his tweed plus fours and made his way down stairs to the gun room. In the gun room he went through the same routine as he did every morning, checking that the rifle was clean, rub off any excess oil, making sure the bolt was operating smoothly and that the scope was well secured. With all the checks complete, and making sure that he had more than enough ammunition, Stuart locked the gun room behind him and went to the kitchen to collect his packed lunch, a packed lunch was standard procedure unless he told the kitchen staff otherwise.

Stuart noticed the unmarked police car as soon as he went out of the back door. The two policemen inside the car were fast asleep. What Stuart didn't notice was the dark people-carrier that was parked at the far end of the car park, nor did he see the blow that struck him just below his left ear. Stuart fell to the ground in a heap.

"Sorry old pal, but I need to borrow your rifle." said Russell aloud but in a low voice. The two sleeping policemen were oblivious as to what had just taken place, right under their noses. Russell walked slowly past their car, shaking his head in a disapproving manner.

Neither Russell, nor anyone else noticed the curtain fall back into place at the window on the third floor of the hotel. What was he to do? He had to get medical help for Mr Brodie without revealing his own identity. He couldn't leave Mr Brodie lying there. He didn't want Mr Brodie seriously hurt or to suffer unnecessarily. He had to waken the two policemen in the car somehow, but how? Then he remembered the technique he had seen Mr Brodie use when he was out on the hills.

Dr Russell slipped quietly out the back door of the hotel. He had a good look around, for he didn't want to be the one accused of assaulting Mr Brodie. There was no one about; even the two policemen were still fast asleep. He knelt down beside the Stuarts limp body and felt a wrist for a pulse. Dr Russell was relieved when he felt a pulse thankfully it was quite strong and steady.

Not far from the police car, the rubbish bins were situated, partly hidden by a privet hedge. The hedge ran the length of the car park and also along the back of the hotel. Between the hedge and the back of the hotel there was a footpath, a path that Dr Russell used frequently. He made his way over to the rubbish bins, concealing himself between the hedge and the bins. From under the hedge he grabbed a handful of stones and dirt and threw these at the rubbish bins. He was hoping that the policemen would waken up, thinking that a dog or cat was rummaging at the bins. It took several handfuls of dirt and stones before one of the policemen woke from his deep sleep. Dr Russell slipped along the path several yards. He was still concealed by the hedge, but able to see the police car.

The policeman got out of the car and stretched, rubbed at his neck and moved his head from side-to-side. Glancing over at the rubbish bins, he was looking for whatever it was that caused him to wake up. It took several more stretches and neck massaging before he noticed the body lying slumped on the ground.

The policeman rubbed at his eyes, making sure what he was seeing was actually there. Realising that his eyes weren't deceiving him, he quickly turned and stuck his head through the open car door.

"Jesus Christ Bob, fucking wake up there's a fucking body lying over there."

As Bob scrambled out of the car, the other policeman made his way over to Stuart's limp body.

"Bob you had better call for an ambulance. This guy seems to be in a bad way."

"Who is it?" Bob asked as he stumbled half way between the police car and where Stuart's body lay. His legs weren't quite functioning properly, after being cramped up in the car all night.

"I think it's that deer stalker chap, Brodie. Just call a fucking ambulance will you?"

"Okay, there's no need to fucking shout" Bob was a bit confused and pissed off now. "Okay Bill, but this won't look good for us, will it? What are we going to say as an excuse?"

"Calling the fucking ambulance and Bob, bring a blanket will you?" Bill patiently tried to get through to Bob, as he put Stuart's body into the recovery position.

Luckily Bob seemed to finally have grasped the urgency of the situation and a minute or so later returned with a blanket.

"Did you call an ambulance?" Bill needed to check.

"Yes, it's on its way. There's a cottage hospital up the road so it should be here in ten minutes or so. What do you think happened to him?"

"I would say by the looks of things, he's been mugged. There's no blood, but going by the swelling on his neck and the back of his head, he's obviously been whacked with something. Have a look in that bag will you?" instructed Bill while he covered Stuart's body with the blanket, tucking it tight underneath him.

"There's a flask, a box of sandwiches, a mobile phone, a pair of binoculars, a knife and a long leather belt."

"No bullets then?" queried Bill.

"No, what makes you think there should be bullets in bag?" asked Bob puzzled.

"Well think about it, the guy's a bloody deer stalker and he was obviously going to work, so what does he use at work? A rifle and there's no rifle to be seen and no bullets."

"Jesus fuck that means whoever mugged him has his fucking rifle and the bullets."

"That's right Bob and where were we when all of this happened?"

"Sleeping in the car" Bob admitted sheepishly.

"No more than thirty feet away and who's turn was it to be on watch?"

"Mine. Sorry Bill."

"You can say that to the Chief, because I'm not taking the blame for this one."

A few minutes later the ambulance crew arrived. They assessed Stuart's condition and decided that it would be best to take him direct to Glasgow. The two policemen followed the ambulance in their car.

Dr Russell waited in the shadows until the ambulance left, and then started the half- hour walk to the seaside, the place where he started from each day. His early morning rendezvous was already waiting for him.

"Good morning sir."

"Can you just give me a moment please?"

"Certainly sir, whenever you are ready."

Dr Russell walked over to his favourite rock the one he sat on every morning and took out his note pad from his rucksack, along with the map. After studying the map for several minutes and jotting down some notes, he returned to the car.

"Where to this morning sir?" said the driver of the car who had been waiting patiently. Dr Russell didn't say a word, he merely handed the driver a piece of paper. Written on the piece of paper was a post code and nothing else.

Inside the car, the driver pressed the appropriate keys on the G.P.S.

"It looks like a two-hour drive sir. Are you quite comfortable?"

"Yes thank you. Wake me up a mile before the destination will you?"

"I certainly will sir."

Dr Russell pressed the reclining lever on the seat, lay back and shut his eyes.

45

Ryan was waiting patiently at the guest house for Stuart. Stuart was already half an hour late. Ryan decided that he would give Stuart another ten minutes and then call him. He was surprised that he hadn't seen John Farrell at breakfast. He did however recall that last night Farrell said that he would be having an early start today, but Ryan hadn't thought Farrell had meant quite so early.

Ten minutes passed, and then Ryan called Stuart's mobile. It rang out several times before a voice said "Hello" Ryan knew straight away that it wasn't Stuart's voice.

"Hello Stuart, its Jim here. Are you still coming round this morning? He said, being cautious.

"This is D.C Dow speaking. I am afraid Stuart Brodie won't be joining you this morning as there has been an incident at the hotel."

"What kind of incident?"

"It appears that Mr Brodie has been assaulted, possibly mugged."

"Is he okay?"

"We're not sure yet, he is still unconscious. He is just on his way to hospital in the ambulance now. What did you say your name was again?"

Ryan didn't reply. He switched off his mobile, not wanting to be recognised.

Ryan got into his car and headed for the Braes of Brackie Hotel, hoping that he would be in time to catch up with the ambulance and follow it to which-ever hospital it took Stuart. As he neared the hotel Ryan could see the ambulance, followed by the unmarked police car about two miles ahead on the coast road, Ryan slowed down allowing them to get even further ahead, he didn't want to be detected. Ryan drove slowly enough so that a car behind him could overtake, helping to shield him from the policemen in front. They were headed towards Glasgow.

Had Hodges finally decided to seek his revenge on Stuart? If so, why wait for so long and why at the hotel? Why didn't Hodges wait until Stuart was away from the hotel, there would be a lesser chance of Hodges being seen or caught and less chance of Stuart being found quickly and taken to hospital. Hodges must have some ulterior motive but what? Then Ryan had a comforting thought maybe Hodges was not confident that he could get at Stuart when Stuart was in his natural element out stalking and Stuart would have a gun at the ready so it would be more dangerous for Hodges. Maybe Hodges was a bit cowardly after all a lot of murders were.

Ryan prayed that Stuart wasn't seriously hurt, for Ryan liked Stuart a lot and was sure that deep down Stuart was a good man. It showed in the way that Stuart cared about nature and the countryside. Yes he shot deer, but as Stuart had explained, it was all part of conservation and for the good of the environment as the natural regeneration of the forests was threatened by a large and expanding deer population. Ryan enjoyed stalking even more as he knew he was not only having fun but helping the environment at the same time. Regarding Stuart's past, Ryan knew that Stuart wasn't squeaky clean. Maybe Stuart had just been in the wrong place at the wrong time and got innocently involve with the wrong people. At this moment Ryan didn't really care about Stuart's past; he just hoped that Stuart would be all right.

At the city hospital, Ryan sat in his car in the car park. Almost an hour passed before the two policemen came out of the hospital. They sat in their car for nearly ten minutes before driving off. Ryan wondered what new instructions they had received, traffic duty, he wouldn't be surprised.

Ryan waited another five minutes before he went into the hospital. At the reception, he asked for Stuart's room number.

Stuart was sitting up in bed, with a bandage around his head holding an ice pack in place. He was looking very sorry for himself. Ryan was relieved he had just spoken to the doctor in the corridor who had told him that Stuart didn't have any serious injuries other than a badly bruised neck and a headache. The doctor said that they would keep Stuart in over-night for observation.

"Hello Stuart. How are you feeling?"

"I suppose I will live." said Stuart as he raised himself further up the bed, wincing at the pain of the exertion.

"What the hell happened?"

"I have no idea. All that I can remember is looking at the two policemen sleeping in their car. The next thing I know I'm in the back of an ambulance with a bloody sore neck and head."

"Do you think it was Russell Hodges that hit you?"

"I am certain it was him, only Russell can deliver a blow with such skill. Depending on the force he uses, it can mean life or death. In my case it's life, thank God, but I will probably have a bloody sore neck for a long time."

"So you don't think he wanted to kill you then? Maybe he was giving you a warning to back off or something?" speculated Ryan.

"No, he didn't want to kill me. If he had wanted to kill me I wouldn't be here sitting talking to you. P.C.s Dumb and Dumber told me just a little while ago, that there was no sign of my rifle or ammunition when they found me so I reckon that's why he whacked me, to get my rifle and if Russell feels the need for a firearm, pity help the next victim."

"But why start using a gun now when he's more than capable with his hands?"

"All I can suggest is that whoever his next target is, he can't get close enough to them, or maybe it's too risky or something and being shot with a .308 sporting bullet, there's not much chance of survival."

"What do you mean by sporting bullet Stuart?"

"Unlike military ammunition, for sports we use soft-nosed bullets that expand on the slightest of impact. If you remember the deer that we shot, there was just a bullet hole on entry, but where the bullet exited there was a hole the size of your fist. A military round, on the other hand, normally goes in and out leaving a similar hole, unless it strikes solid bone. Hollow points are even more lethal. Apart from .22 rim fires, they are illegal in the military and for deer stalking" explained Stuart.

"Did the two great detectives say anything else? They must be quite anxious, especially with a firearm and ammunition being stolen" Ryan asked.

"They seem to be putting it down to some sort of mugging. They did ask me if I had seen a dark blue people carrier, as the local milkman said he had seen an unknown vehicle earlier on. But as I told you, all I saw were the two sleeping beauties. So where do we go from here?"

Ryan didn't answer Stuart, for he was deep in thought. "Are you okay Ryan you look like you have just seen that ghost again?"

"Sorry, I was just thinking. Tell me Stuart what does Russell Hodges look like?" Ryan sounded worried.

"Don't you already know, surely his photo is on file?"

"I am sure it is but it is in a classified file that I don't have access too" replied Ryan dryly.

"Oh I didn't realise, well, he's about the same height, build and age as myself, has fair hair, usually cropped, he has lightish blue eyes and I suppose he's quite a handsome chap in his own way. Oh and when I knew him he had a healthy tan but who knows if he still does after his time in prison. Why do you ask?"

"I think I had dinner with him last night. He was staying at the same guest house, posing as an insurance salesman and he drove a dark blue people-carrier. Damn it, I knew there was something not quite right about him, but I just couldn't put my finger on it. Shit, if only I'd realised at the time, I could have had him and you wouldn't be lying here."

Stuart tried to console him "That could be true, but then you might be in the bed next to me or worse, had you gone up against Russell. That is something that you don't want to do on your own, believe me"

"Damn it, I should have known. There I was having dinner with the most wanted man in Britain and I didn't even fucking know it. Christ, Hodges must think I am a right fucking dick. Well he won't be back there, that's for sure, because he knew that I was a policeman straight away, unlike me. Shit, maybe I should join Blake's outfit of incompetents or take early retirement."

"There's no point in blaming yourself. You have to remember that Russell's as cunning as any bloody fox and a very dangerous one at that. He will do what he has to do and no-one or nothing will stop him. He's literally what you might call a lean, mean killing machine. Only a bullet will stop him and that won't be easy. Christ, he's been following me for days in the big wood and yesterday out on the bloody hill and all I can manage is to catch a glimpse of him and now he has my rifle and you feel bad?"

"You say he was out on the hill yesterday?"

"Yes he was spying on me using binoculars. The sun was reflecting off them. Come to think of it, he probably did that deliberately so I would notice him."

"What time did you see him on the hill at Stuart?"

"It would be round about one o'clock, early afternoon"

"How long do you think it would take him to get from where you saw him, to the guest house where I am staying?"

"Well, from where I saw him, it would take him a good three hours to reach a main road, depending on which road he was parked off, mind you, there are only two. Even if he parked on either one, it would still take him at least an hour to drive to where you are staying."

"So, if you saw him leave the hill at say one thirty and it took him three hours to reach his car and then an hour's drive to the guest house, altogether that's four hours and giving him time to change his clothes, he would arrive at the guest house around five forty-five, which is exactly the time the would-be sales rep arrived" Ryan said piecing it all together "Damn, if only I had known."

"Well like I said earlier Ryan, it's probably for the best that you didn't know" assured Stuart.

"Right, I am going to call my governor and tell him what's happened, see if he can push things on so we can make some arrests before Russell kills everybody. I will call him now. Is there anything I can get you while I am out Stuart?"

"No thanks. I am fine just now."

Ryan left the room leaving Stuart with his thoughts, what a bloody mess and I thought this was all behind me. I feel like an animal that's just been stalked, but then, they don't normally live to tell the tale. "Thanks for sparing my life you bastard, but I will get you, don't you worry about that." said Stuart aloud as he drifted off into sleep, taking his thoughts with him.

186

46

The Factor met with Catherine Blake and two businessmen for lunch at a hotel in the centre of Glasgow.

"We have a very big problem. Not only do we have a hit-man out to get us, but also a fucking cop from London sniffing around. So what are we going to do about it?" demanded the Factor.

"I had D.S. Jones recalled to London but he came back, apparently he is now on holiday. I told him that if he interferes in any police work whatsoever he will be arrested. I've got two of my boys watching him just in case and if he so much as parks on a double yellow line, they will have him" said Blake pretending that she had everything under control.

"Oh and so why is my deer stalker in hospital if your boys are on the ball?" sniped the Factor.

"It is Jones they are watching not Brodie" said Blake not letting on that her boys had lost Jones's trail days ago. "But on that point Peter, Jones seems to have befriended your deer stalker Stuart Brodie for some reason, which I find a little bit odd considering that Brodie was a suspect in the Asian murders"

"What do you mean he was a suspect, for what?" the Factor is surprised and not pleased.

"Do you remember when your man Maynard was killed in Asia? Stuart Brodie was there; in fact he was arrested for Maynard's murder. They obviously didn't have enough evidence against him because he got bail and came back here. God only knows who else he met out there anyway his name kept cropping up in these latest murders and that's why D.S. Jones got in touch with you" explained Catherine

"Christ if I had known this, I would never have taken him back on the estate. You mean to tell me that Stuart Brodie might have actually killed Rick Maynard, who at the time was our main man in Asia?" retorted the Factor

"Whether he killed him or not, Stuart must know a lot more than he's letting on and that's why D.S. Jones has befriended him. Listen there's a lot at stake here and I for one am not about to lose everything just because of some would-be Sherlock Holmes from London and a bloody deer stalker. They have to go, it's the only solution" Blake was getting angry.

"And what about the hit man, do you think he's working with this deer stalker chap of yours Peter?" asked Jim Forsyth, one of the so-called business men.

Catherine answered for the Factor "I don't think so, but were not going to take any chances. I think that this hit-man whoever he is has been hired by one of our rivals abroad. We know who the hit man is, well sort of. After Maynard was murdered if you remember, two of his men were killed after they murdered a David Philips. Then Philip's cousin as a reprisal killed two of Maynard's men. The whole situation had got out of control and if you remember disrupted our organisation for months"

"Yes" said the businessman ruefully "I lost a packet"

Catherine continued "The cousin then spent two or three years in jail but was eventually released on bail. The London C.I.D. think the cousin is now in the U.K, out for revenge against anyone that was connected with Maynard. His name is Russell Hodges, but he is obviously using an assumed name or we would have picked him up by now."

"Damn it Catherine, why in hell's name wasn't I told about this before now?" the Factor was furious.

"Sorry Peter, I thought we would handle it I didn't want to bother you with minor details"

"Minor details, Christ Catherine, we've got a bloody assassin picking us off one by one, a cop from London sniffing around and one of my own deer stalkers in bloody hospital and only God knows what he knows and you tell me that you didn't want to bother me with minor fucking details? Well I suggest you get it sorted quick, before it's too late, after all that's what you're paid for. As for you two, get another couple of your lads to take care of Jones and Brodie. I don't care how you do it, just get it done. On second thoughts, leave Jones to me. I have someone that can sort him out and Catherine, get every man you can spare out looking for this chap Hodges, or whatever he calls himself okay?"

They all assured the Factor that they would see to it. The Factor and Catherine Blake remained seated as the other two got up and left the restaurant with their tails between their legs. They were totally unaware that as soon as they stepped outside the building, they were followed.

47

Ryan returned to Stuart's bedside after having had a lengthy discussion with his boss. Stuart had fallen asleep while Ryan had been gone. He wakened quickly when Ryan entered the room, startled by the sudden noise, not that it was loud, it was more the fact that Stuart's nerves were a bit frayed.

"How are you feeling now, any better?" enquired Ryan.

"Yes I am actually. I had a good sleep while you were out. I've still got a sore neck though."

Ryan can't hide his excitement as he tells Stuart about his talk with his boss. "Well Stuart, I had a good chat with my Guv and told him what's happened. He told me, that the Secret Service is onto this. Catherine Blake has been under a bit of suspicion, for quite some time. Now that they know the Factor's the main man, they're getting ready for a bust. They're going to bring in the flying squad and try to hit every place at the same time. I am meeting two of them at your Factor's office tomorrow morning and that I can't wait just to see the look on the Factor's face when we arrest him."

"Wish I could be there to see it, not that I have a personal grudge other than the fact that he is Britain's biggest drug dealer" joked Stuart, a bit weak but at least he was trying to be up-beat.

"Stuart, I have got some things to get ready for tomorrow, is there anything I can get for you before I go?"

"No thanks, I am okay and good luck for tomorrow." "Thanks, I will let you know how things go. Take it easy Stuart and I will see you tomorrow at some point."

"I don't have much choice other than to take it easy" replies Stuart ruefully.

Ryan left leaving Stuart helpless in bed and that's just the way Stuart felt. Stuart lay in bed feeling sorry for himself, annoyed that he couldn't go with Ryan and join in the excitement, not that he could do anything to help anyway. After all it had nothing to do with him really, it just so happened that he was caught up in the middle of things, purely by chance. Or was it?

There seemed to be too many coincidences for Stuart's liking. His past in Asia had returned to haunt him but there couldn't be any connection between Rick Maynard and the Factor, could there? If not, it was a bit of a co-incidence that he had met Rick in Asia or was it? If Rick was connected to the Factor and the drugs ring maybe Rick knew Stuart was on his way to Asia and deliberately hooked up with him. Maybe, initially just to find out what was going on at the Scottish end of the operation and then Rick had found out that Stuart could be useful.

Russell was a murdering psychopath that liked to kill drug dealers for money Rick was a drug dealer that explains the link with Russell.

But at the moment Stuart's immediate concern was that a murdering psychopath, Russell, was running loose with a rifle, his rifle.

48

The two business men left the restaurant on foot, unaware that they were being followed. They walked for twenty minutes or so before they stopped at the entrance to a multi-storey car park. They were both quite agitated as they chatted.

Russell stopped ten yards short of them and took out his mobile phone, pretending that he had just received a text message. The street was very busy with lots of traffic and people coming and going, not taking any notice of each other. There was no need for Russell to hide as he blended in rather well with the unconcerned masses who seemed focused only on their own missions, whatever they might be.

Russell leaned against the wall keeping a close eye on the two would-be business men. There was too much noise to hear what they were talking about and too many passers-by obstructing his view to lip read. All he could do was wait.

Russell decided to go into the multi storey-car park, as he was certain at least one of them had a car parked there. He moved towards the entrance of the car park and was then close enough to hear one say to the other, "My car is in here. I can drop you off. It's no problem."

Russell slipped in behind them as they made their way into the car park, his luck was in.

Russell kept his head low as he walked. Conscious of the C.C.T.V monitors, he just hoped there wouldn't be too many inside. It was an un-manned car park; the barrier was operated by a card system and to Russell's surprise there were no other cameras, only the ones at the entrance. The two drug-dealing business men headed towards the rear of the first level. The car park was full up. There seemed to be no empty spaces at all. The lights on the walls were very dim and the air was stifled by carbon monoxide. An adequate place for these rats to die, thought Russell.

The two men stopped next to a silver Range Rover gabbling on about the Factor, cursing him. Russell was no longer interested in what they had to say as he was now in stealth mode. Within a few seconds, Russell confronted the two men as they stood at the rear of the Range Rover. He took a quick glance around the garage, checking that no one was about.

"What the f...?" were the last words that came from the mouth of the first man who received a lethal blow to the neck. The other man who was rendered speechless just stood with his mouth open in disbelief and horror. A second later, he too lay on the floor, lifeless.

Russell quickly dragged the two bodies out of sight between the Range Rover and the car parked next to it. One of the men made a slight groaning noise, probably caused by escaping gasses from his stomach. To be on the safe side, Russell was going to make sure that they were dead.

He didn't bother checking them for a pulse, just rolled them over onto their stomachs. Russell took the slim, two-inched curved blade from his pocket, grasped the first one by the back of his hair and forced the head forward. He inserted the sharp blade between the skull and first vertebrae and with a twitch of the wrist the body gave a slight shudder as the spinal cord was severed, relaxing muscles and nerves. Russell carried out the same procedure on the second body and then he removed their mobile phones, for if they rang, it could draw the attention of a passer-by to stop and take a closer look.

Russell then pushed the corpses under the Range Rover as far as he could. With a bit of luck, their bodies wouldn't be discovered for several hours.

Russell casually walked out of the car park, blanking the C.C.T.V. and joined the bustling crowd out on the street.

Another job done without even breaking sweat and with no-one any the wiser, just the way Russell liked it.

49

George was on his patrol of the multi storey car park. It was his last port of call before his shift finished. He worked part-time for a local security company ever since he had retired from the police force, just as many ex-policemen did. It helped to keep them active as well as giving them a small extra income. His hours were from ten pm to six am three nights a week. The multi-storey car park was one of four that he checked twice during the night. For five years, George had been making the same routine checks. In the five years in the job, George had never encountered any trouble whatsoever.

Over the years, George had got to know every vehicle that parked overnight in the car park. He was quite surprised to see the silver Range Rover still there, as it wasn't a regular 'sleeper' as he called them. Having an avid interest in cars, George sauntered over to the Range Rover for a closer look. It was the latest model. After admiring the interior of the vehicle, George stepped back a few paces to the side. It was only then, that George noticed the bulky shape underneath the Range Rover. After a closer inspection, George was horrified at the gruesome discovery of the two bodies crammed under the car.

It wasn't long before the C.I.D. were on the scene. They quickly identified the two bodies and notified Superintendent Catherine Blake. The dark green-coloured Jaguar came speeding out of the drive way and headed north east from Glasgow. Catherine Blake was in a bit of a hurry, spooked by the phone call she had received earlier, informing her about the double murder of her business associates. "I have to get out" she thought "or I will be next, God what a mess, why can't we catch this bloody murderer? I need police protection myself now. I wish I had never got involved in all this, but Peter was so charming and it seemed easy money. But we have had to kill so many people, that poor woman Sharon as if it wasn't bad enough that we had to kill her husband, years ago, when he found out too much, then we had to kill her too, just because men can't keep it in their trousers. Those poor children, I do feel guilty. Perhaps when this is all over I can do something for them a charitable donation? Yes, that will make me feel better" Blake's thoughts were feverish.

"I'll go to Peter and hide out at his farm till this is over and Hodges is caught. I will tell work that I am ill from stress, woman's problems that always works and I need complete rest"

Catherine began to feel more cheerful as she formulated her plans. "Things will work out, they always have even when we lost Maynard years ago we got back on our feet and we will survive this as well."

She wasn't aware of the black people-carrier that was following her.

Russell's information had been correct.

50

Ryan had an early breakfast and went for a walk as he had several hours to kill before meeting with the two secret service men.

His walk took him along the river banks. It all seemed quite mystical. The river itself was slow moving, not that much of it was visible, for there was a blanket of mist covering the entire surface, about four feet thick. Along the banks of the river, alder and willow trees grew, some of which over hung the river, their branches disappearing into the blanket of mist below. Ryan was amazed at the sight; it as if he was a character in one of the old Hammer House of Horror movies when at any time he could expect to see a ghoulish figure appear from within the depths of the mist.

A few hundred yards further on, Ryan found himself walking on a path that lead into Brackie village. In the village, there wasn't much sign of life other than the milkman making his early-morning delivery to the local shop. What a wonderful place to get away from it all, thought Ryan.

No doubt the local people would be completely shocked once news of the Factor's arrest got out. The scandal would give them something to gossip about for months to come, maybe even years.

Ryan walked through the village and entered the gates that led to a large house belonging to the estate. The house was a very impressive building, a small stately home. In the same way as many houses of the period and as with many of the private estates throughout Britain, its doors and grounds had been opened to the public in order to help meet with the costs of the up-keep of the house and its policies.

Ryan and his wife had visited many such places in the south of England, when their daughter was young. It was the lavish landscaped gardens that his wife had been interested in, rather than the buildings. Had she still been alive, Ryan would certainly have brought her to Scotland for a holiday, but sadly it wasn't to be. Ryan found himself taking a bigger interest in such places, now that he was on his own as it gave him some connection to his dead wife. He was still sad and distressed about her death but Ryan was beginning to accept and find comfort in the thought that she was watching over him.

Around the big house as the locals called it, there were driveways and footpaths leading in all directions. These were flanked by avenues of large oak and lime trees interlaced with rhododendrons and shrubs.

Ryan made his way down a drive which was sign-posted 'Office Authorised Personnel Only'. On reaching the building, Ryan was suitably impressed with the structure, for it too was a rather grand building. The building had once been the coach house and stables and it was still in its original state, just as it had been for centuries. Only now it was one of the estate offices, the nerve centre for the day-to-day running of the affairs in this part of the estate, but as people would soon find out, the man in charge of the whole estate was not only their Factor, but also the mastermind of the biggest drug operation in the U.K.

What a perfect setup, thought Ryan, but not for much longer, as the Factor's empire was about to come crashing down. With only a few hours to go before the Factor's demise, Ryan headed back towards the guest house to collect his belongings and car, for this was one rendezvous he didn't want to be late for.

51

Stuart sat in the hospital foyer waiting for Steve who was on the way to pick him up and take him back to the hotel. Stuart was feeling quite good apart from a bit of a sore neck. The doctor had given Stuart the all-clear after a routine check. He said he was satisfied with Stuart's condition and that Stuart could go home.

Stuart was keen to get out of the hospital. Although he had been looked-after well enough, he didn't want to stay there any longer than need be. He wasn't sure what it was that made him feel uncomfortable, whether it was the smell of cleanliness, the noise, or maybe the fact that he felt like a fraudster taking up a bed when he knew there were people in greater need of one than himself.

Stuart was wondering how the day's events would turn out, what with the Factor and his disciples about to be arrested.   How will it affect everyone's jobs on the estate? It was certainly going to 'upset the apple cart' for a while, to say the least. Maybe he should move on to pastures new and put all of the past behind him once and for all, thought Stuart, but he knew within his own mind that the past would always be there lurking, just waiting to rear its ugly head.

Stuart considered the thought of a holiday for he hadn't been away since his return from Asia. Some holiday that had turned out to be, it had been more like a nightmare. Although it hadn't been all bad he supposed, for he had seen a part of the world that was quite unique.

The culture and its people who seemed to want to be part of western civilisation, desperate to please and ever-so-humble. They would share with you whatever they had, no matter how little it was, whether it is food or their homes, anything at all, even their daughters. Just striving for a better life; a life that most of them would never have or experience, they were to be exploited, not only in the sweat shops or in prostitution, but also drug-trafficking. Some had no choice in the matter due to Mafia tactics. Others would be drawn in by the riches and the chance of a better life-style and more often than not, the consequences would be devastating.

Stuart knew only too well how easy it was to be duped and become involved with something that you didn't particularly want to be involved in but quite often the realisation comes just that little bit too late for some. Stuart felt no regrets about his part in helping rid society of the hardened drug dealers, but as the saying goes, if you play with fire, it's only a matter of time before you get burned.

Maybe a more conventional holiday would be the answer, somewhere with plenty of sun and nothing much to do other than sit around all day watching and listening to people enjoying and making a fool of themselves. Not that they mind making a fool of themselves, they are on holiday and want to make the most of it. No, thought Stuart, that type of holiday wasn't for him as he didn't care for lying on a beach all day or lounging around a swimming pool with masses of people. Maybe he would just stay at home and sort out the garden, or better still take a trip down south and visit the kids. He decided that's just what he would do, once things settled back to normal.

Stuart had to admit he was puzzled by Russell's behaviour, Stuart had thought he knew how Russell's mind worked. He had spent almost a year with him in Asia and after spending that amount of time with Russell, Stuart believed he knew him well and that there was something more than just a bond between himself and Russell, they had been through such a lot together.

On more than one occasion they had saved each others lives, not to mention taking the lives of others and that's where the bond begins or ends. Loyalty and trust are the key ingredients to such a relationship.

Had Russell possibly flipped? Maybe he had been in the jungle for too long? With all that heat, always on full-alert, always looking over his shoulder and the constant killing. Not that the killing seemed to bother Russell, in fact he was in his element when on a mission. Even when they weren't on a mission, Russell never seemed restless or agitated in any way. He just took everything in his stride, a true professional. When Russell got word of a new target, he would quite calmly say, "Pack up, we're on the move." And that's what kept puzzling Stuart, for Russell operates only through instruction and if he's true to form, then who is pulling the strings?

Stuart knew that the Asian government had hired Russell, but surely they wouldn't send him on a mission outside their own country. Maybe it was a personal vendetta that had brought Russell to the U.K. for Stuart knew Russell spent a lot of time with his cousin, who had a very attractive girlfriend, Russell seemed close to them both, so perhaps after all the family bond was strong enough to make Russell flip.

Stuart now sat rubbing the side of his head. He had developed a serious headache brought on through racking his brain in search of answers. All he wanted to do now was lie down and sleep.

"Are you all right Mr Brodie?" Asked the young nurse who had walked over from reception. She must have noticed the discomfort that Stuart was feeling.

"Yes, I am fine thanks. I've just got a bit of a headache that's all."

"Can I get you something for it?"

"Yes, I wouldn't mind if you could."

"Of course I can. Just give me a minute and I will be right back."

"Thanks." said Stuart, as he tried to muster a smile.

The nurse returned with Stuart's pills and at the same time Steve entered the foyer and strolled over to where Stuart was seated. As he did so all heads turned to stare at him, patients and nurses, they were obviously surprised at the sight of the new-comer. They probably didn't see many six and a half foot hairy giants in Glasgow.

"Hello Stuart how are you doing?"

"Hi Steve, I am fine."

"Have you come to take Mr Brodie home?" asked the young nurse who's wide eyed gaze was now firmly fixed on Steve.

"Yes, that's if he wants to." said Steve, giving the young nurse a rather coy smile.

"I am Julie by the way" said the young nurse then she blushed at being so forward.

"Hello Julie, I'm Steve" said Steve taking her hand and attempting to turn on the charm.

"Ready when you are" Stuart interrupted the moment.

"Well goodbye Mr Brodie you take care of yourself okay?" said Julie

"I will, don't you worry and if I don't then I am sure Steve here will be only to glad to bring me back." said Stuart seeing chemistry working between the nurse and Steve.

"It was nice meeting you Steve."

"And you, Julie!"

The blossoming romance was all too much for Stuart. He started walking towards the door leaving Steve behind, still chatting, transfixed by the young nurse.

Stuart waited impatiently at Steve's truck for almost ten minutes before Steve arrived back.

"You took your bloody time didn't you?"

"Sorry Stuart."

They drove in silence for a good ten minutes, heading out of Glasgow.

"Okay, so how did you get on with, Julie?" Stuart had got over his pique.

"Great, she's a lovely girl."

"And?" prompted Stuart.

"She gave me her phone number, said to give her a call the next time I am in Glasgow."

"And that will be next week I suppose?"

"If not before." said Steve grinning widely.

Stuart just shook his head.

"By the way Stuart, did you hear about the two murders?"

"What murders?" Stuart was fully alert again at hearing the latest news.

"I heard about them on the radio as I was coming to fetch you. Apparently a car park attendant found two bodies stuffed under a Range Rover in a multi- storey here in Glasgow.

"When did he find them?"

"Early this morning I think they said."

"Did they say on the news how they were killed?"

"Yes, apparently they had been stabbed in the back of the neck."

"Did it say who they were?"

"No, just that they were two businessmen from Glasgow. The place is becoming like a bloody war zone. I mean even look at what happened to you yesterday, you might have been killed as well."

"You're right there Steve and the bastard that whacked me has my rifle."

"Shit, I forgot all about your rifle being stolen Stuart. It wasn't the Manlicher was it?"

"No it was my .308, even so, that's bad enough."

"Yes I suppose it is. Whoever jumped you must have been waiting for you."

"It would seem that way. Keep your ears open Steve in case you hear of anybody that's just acquired a new rifle, or is selling one, you never know."

"I certainly will Mr Brodie." said Steve with a grin. Stuart knew exactly where Steve's thoughts were. That suited Stuart fine for he had his own to think about.

Stuart's wondered about the two bodies that were found under the Range Rover. It was definitely Russell's handy work. At least Russell hadn't started using the rifle yet. A shiver ran down Stuart's spine at his next thought; what if Russell was saving the rifle for their inevitable confrontation, the grand finale?

52

Catherine Blake's Jaguar sped along the country roads still heading north east. Russell held back not wanting to frighten the superintendent any more than she already was although Russell doubted whether Blake would even bother checking her rear view mirror, for she was in such a hurry. She was a desperate woman on the run. Events were working out well for Russell, for he knew exactly where Catherine Blake was headed.

Christine arrived at the estate office as punctual as ever. She liked to be in before the Factor and the other staff. It was her daily routine that had spanned fifty years. She parked her Morris Minor in the usual spot next to where the Factor parked his Range Rover. As Christine was unlocking the heavy oak door that led into the office, a dark green Jaguar pulled up beside her car. Christine turned round to scrutinise the car and driver.

"Hello Mrs Blake, I haven't seen you in a long time, are you here to see Peter?"

"Hello Christine, yes I am, will he be long?"

"No he won't be long, would you like to come inside and wait?"

"Yes if that's okay."

"Of course it is, come in and I will make you a nice cup of tea. Oh, but before you come in Mrs Blake, do you think you could move your car over to the visitors parking area?" "Yes of course I can." said Blake, who was taken aback slightly at the request, but then thought, why not?

She enforced the same parking procedures at her own office. She moved her car and went inside.

Christine had already made her a cup of tea and placed it on the table next to the old leather couch which had seen better days. On the table there were various magazines mostly about shooting and fishing.

"Here you are Mrs Blake. If you will take a seat here just now until Peter arrives"

"Thank you Christine."

Twenty minutes passed during which time Catherine Blake had flicked through all of the magazines that lay on the table, she had not taken much notice of their contents as her mind was deep in thought elsewhere.

"Here's Peter now, Mrs Blake."

Blake looked around the room for a CCTV monitor, or something to indicate the Factor's arrival, for she hadn't heard any vehicle whatsoever and there were no windows looking out to the parking area. The old bat must have super-sonic hearing.

The Factor entered the office.

"Good morning Christine."

"Good morning Peter. Mrs Blake is here to see you"

"Ah Catherine, another new car I see. Come through to my office. Christine will you hold any calls for me meantime, please?"

The Factor walked into his office followed by Blake. "Shut the door Catherine. Now what in God's name are you doing here?"

"I am scared Peter. I need to get away now before it's too late."

"What do you mean before it's too late? Listen, once Jones and Brodie have been taken care of and this hit man, whoever he is, is caught, everything will be back the way it was. So don't panic, just relax and be patient. There's too much at stake."

"That's just it, I am panicking. You obviously didn't hear the news this morning did you?"

"No I didn't, why, what has happened?"

"Martin and Jim have been murdered, their bodies were found early this morning, crammed under Martin's Range Rover in the multi-storey car park. It looks like they were killed not long after they left us at the restaurant."

"Christ, that means whoever killed them must have followed them from the restaurant and killed them in broad daylight"

"Now do you see why we need to get away, until this is all sorted out? This killer is a professional, for Martin and Jim were no pushovers they were bloody hard men and I don't want to be next."

"Maybe the killer isn't working alone" said the Factor.

"It doesn't matter Peter if he's alone or not, none of us are safe. He's obviously done his homework on us, or been well informed by someone who knows about our operation. The only solution that I can think of is to get the hell out of here" Catherine felt the beginnings of hysteria.

"So what are you planning to do now Catherine? I mean, why have you come here? You could have told me all of this over the telephone" the Factor was curt and unsympathetic.

"I thought it would be better if I told you face-to-face about what has happened. Besides, I just had to get away from Glasgow. Shit I am actually scared Peter, do you know that? Here I am the head of Glasgow Police Force and I can't do a bloody thing about what's happening."

"So what is your plan then?" the Factor asked again.

"Well I was thinking that maybe we could both go to your farm it is well protected or get the hell out of the country and go to your villa in Spain. If we stick together we might have a better chance of seeing this through and maybe find out who's behind these murders and why? So what do you think?"

The Factor was quiet for several minutes, deep in thought.

"Okay here's what we'll do. I think we are better to get out of Scotland for now. I will tell Christine that I have to go away for a few days on urgent business. We will go to my house and I will pack a few things. You can leave your car in my garage. I don't think it would be a good idea to fly from any of the Scottish airports, just in case, so what we'll do is drive down to London and get the first available flight to Spain. Once we're there, we'll see about recruiting some new people and try and get this mess sorted. Damn it, everything was going so well until this lunatic came on the scene"

"Maybe it's time to give it up Peter, you know retire? I am sure you must have made a bundle by now."

"That's not the point Catherine. Some bastard's out to get us and I want to know who and why. Right just give me a few minutes and then we'll go."

The Factor had just started to rise from his seat when there was a knock at the door.

"Yes." said the Factor, expecting Christine to walk in through the door. The Factor couldn't hide his shock as Ryan Jones and the two secret service men walked into his office. A deathly silence fell upon the room.

Christine pushed her way past Ryan and the two secret service men.

"I am sorry Peter. I asked these gentlemen to wait in the reception but they just walked on through."

"That's okay Christine, don't worry, everything's all right. I will give you a call if we need anything."

"Peter Grant and Catherine Blake, we are arresting you on suspicion of drug-trafficking, fraud, money-laundering and conspiracy to commit murder. You do not have to say anything but it may harm your defence if you withhold something you later rely upon in court."

"Just wait a bloody minute here Jones. I have already told you that you have no jurisdiction here and what are you talking about?" demanded Blake.

"These two gentlemen are from the secret service. They have had you under surveillance for quite some time. They know everything about your operation. The game is over. Now we can do this the easy way or the hard way it's up to you" explained Ryan.

"I want to call my lawyer." said the Factor, who had now realised that they were in deep shit.

"Sure, go ahead Mr Grant. You can tell him or her that you are being taken to police head quarters in Edinburgh. What about you Mrs Blake, do you want to call your lawyer?" asked Ryan, enjoying every minute of their demise. They weren't so high and mighty now, more like two school-kids who had just been caught behind the bike sheds up to no good by the headmaster. The Factor in particular was looking of shamefaced and embarrassed.

"No I don't want a lawyer because I haven't done anything wrong. You are making a big mistake here Jones and I will personally see to it that you are kicked out of the police force" said Catherine Blake trying desperately hard to sound believable.

The Factor made a phone call to his lawyer explaining the situation in a calm and confident manner.

"Okay, now turn around and put your hands behind your backs" instructed Ryan.

"Christ you don't have to bloody handcuff us do you?" complained the Factor.

"I am afraid so. We don't want you trying to make a run for it, now do we?" answered Ryan.

"You're a real bastard Jones, you know that?" said Catharine Blake in a venomous voice.

"Just doing my job, now turn around" replied Ryan feigning disinterest.

The two secret service men put the handcuffs on Catherine and the Factor and led them out of the office.

"Oh Peter, what on earth's going on?" said Christine as she stood behind her desk, rubbing her withered hands together, concerned and puzzled.

"There is nothing to worry about Christine; it's just a big misunderstanding that's all. I would appreciate it if you could keep this to yourself Christine and if anyone asks for me today, tell them that I am away on business, okay? I will give you a call later on today and don't worry, everything will be fine" the Factor reassured Christine.

The Factor and Blake were led outside by the two secret service men. The prisoners were held by their arms. Ryan Jones followed at the rear.

Outside it was a beautiful morning. The sun was shining and there was a very slight, but warm breeze. It was perfect harvesting weather. Everyone seemed to pause for a moment taking in the fresh late summer air when one of the secret service men's mobile phones rang.

As he answered, he stepped away from his captive. Suddenly there was an almighty boom and another sound like a muffled explosion. The two secret service men seemed to fall away from their captives. Ryan Jones for a moment thought that there had been a gas explosion or a water main had burst, for he felt the sensation of something splattering across his face. Whatever it was, it felt hot and jagged. Ryan heard a second blast and felt a sudden burning sensation in his neck and that was it.

The first bullet had struck the Factor on the bridge of his nose, causing his head to disintegrate, like a ripe tomato exploding. His legs gave way and his lifeless body slumped backwards, falling to the ground. His head, or what was left of it, came to rest on the hard surface, with a sound not unlike that of a wet sponge being dropped on a floor. Catherine Blake took the second bullet square in the middle of her chest, shattering bones, sending them in all directions through the large hole in her back. As the .308 bullet ripped through her body, it was a piece of her bone, blasted into shrapnel that had struck Jones in his neck.

A few minutes passed. No more shots were fired. The two secret service men looked across to each other and rose to their feet.

"Are you okay?" asked one to the other.

"Yes I am fine, what about you?"

"I'm okay. But shit! Jones is down. Call an ambulance quick."

He rushed over to where Ryan Jones's apparently lifeless body lay. Blood was oozing out of the wound in Ryan's neck as Ryan was checked for vital signs. He was alive. The Secret Service man took a handkerchief from his pocket and put it to the wound on Ryan's neck, applying as much pressure as he could in an attempt to stem the flow of blood. It was only then that he looked over at the bodies of the Factor and Blake.

"What a fucking mess." he said aloud as he took in the gory scene that lay before him.

Meanwhile, his colleague ushered Christine back into the office. She had been standing at the door, with one hand clasped over her mouth, the other gripping her cardigan tightly around her neck. She was in total shock at what she had witnessed. "Come on love, go back inside. We need an ambulance here and quick" said the Secret Service man gently.

After calling for an ambulance, the Secret Service man asked Christine if she had any blankets or towels. Christine didn't reply she just sat there, still gripping her cardigan tightly, staring vacantly into space. The Secret Service man took her coat from the hat and coat stand that stood in the far corner of the room. He gently placed it around Christine's shoulders.

"You'll be fine love, the ambulance is on its way." he said reassuringly. In the toilets he found several towels which he took outside and covered the top half of the two corpses. He removed the handcuffs. He also gave a towel to his colleague who was tending to Ryan Jones. His colleague replaced the blood-soaked handkerchief with the towel. In the distance the wail of the ambulance siren could be heard.

53

It was midday by the time Stuart and Steve reached
the Braes of Brackie Hotel. Stuart decided that he would
stay the night at the hotel as he didn't feel quite up to the
long drive home. Stuart thought he would just relax, maybe
have a bath and enjoy a good dinner. Steve said that he
would come round later and join him as Steve wasn't in any
rush to get home either. Stuart was also hoping that Ryan
would drop by and give him a run-down on the day's
activities.

After having had a good soak in the bath and a few
hours sleep, Stuart felt quite refreshed and somewhat
hungry, for he hadn't eaten anything since the bowl of
porridge for breakfast in the hospital. He got dressed and
made his way to the restaurant. Much to his surprise, Steve
was sitting at the bar.

"Hello Steve. I didn't expect to see you here so
soon."

"Bloody hell Stuart, have I got some news to tell
you." said Steve who looked very troubled. "What do you
want to drink Stuart?"

"Nothing just now thanks Steve."

"I think you better have a drink Stuart, because you'll
need one after I tell you what has happened."

"Okay then, I will have a pint of Guinness. Now
what's the news?" asked Stuart, who had a good inkling
about Steve's news. It would be news of the Factor's arrest.

"I will tell you in minute. Let's sit over there" said Steve.

Stuart got his pint of Guinness and they went over to one of the leather couches by the fire.

"The Factor was killed this morning, right outside the fucking office, shot, apparently blew his head clean off. Two policemen were shot as well. One of them was splattered all over the place; the other one's still alive, just. Poor old Christine saw it all happen. She's in the hospital as well, suffering from shock" Steve explained in a rush.

Stuart was dumbfounded, this was not what he had expected, he immediately thought about Ryan, was Ryan okay "Who were the policemen that were shot, do you know?" Stuart asked urgently.

"Yes, the one who was splattered all over the place was the head of Glasgow police. The other one, as far as I know, was from London. I don't know what the hell was going on. All I have heard is that it wasn't a pretty sight, blood and guts and the Factor's brains all over the place. Christ! I have just had a thought Stuart. Do you think it could be the same guy that knocked you out and stole your rifle?"

"I don't know Steve; it could be from what you say about the damage done. A shot with a .308 would certainly make a hell of a mess. Do you know which hospital they took Christine and the policeman to?" Stuart was eager to find out if the injured policeman was Ryan.

"Glasgow I think. Do you want another pint Stuart?"

"Yes okay. You were right about needing a drink after hearing this."

Steve got up and went to the bar for more drinks. Stuart immediately phoned the Glasgow hospital and asked if a D.S. Ryan Jones had been admitted, he had been and was in quite a serious condition. Stuart hoped that Ryan was going to be alright. He would go visit Ryan first thing in the morning.

Stuart was furious with Russell. Yes Russell you bastard, I will get you for this. Why did you shoot Ryan? And, you might have at least waited until everyone was away from the office before killing them. Poor Christine will never be the same again after witnessing the shootings. Steve arrived back with the drinks, sat down and shook his head.

"I don't know what's going on around here anymore. First Sharon gets killed, then those two guys in the lay by, then you get whacked and your rifle stolen and now this happens. I mean, what's it all about Stuart? Who would want to do this? Is there just some fucking nutter out there going around killing people for kicks or what?"

"I don't know Steve. I suppose we'll find out soon enough. Let's go to the bar and see if there's anything on the news about it"

Just as they sat down at the bar, Stuart received a text message "Come and find me tomorrow." it read. The sender's number was withheld but Stuart knew straight away who the text was from. Okay Russell, I will come and play your games with you.

The headlines on the local news were very dramatic: "brutal slayings on private estate in rural Scotland. The motive behind the brutal murders is not yet known. All that is known at present is that the estate Factor and a top policeman from Glasgow were shot dead outside the estate office, along with a policeman from London, who was fortunate and is stable in hospital. A major manhunt is underway to catch the assailant. The Factor's personal secretary is also in hospital being treated for shock. She allegedly witnessed the shootings."

The next news item caught Stuart's attention it concerns a raid of a farm in the Highlands and many arrests in Glasgow and the West coast. According to the news reader this was this result of a year long investigation into an international drug ring. "Good" though Stuart "at least the drug ring closed down"

"I would love to get my hands on the bastard that did in the Factor" said Steve.

"You're not the only one" replied Stuart absently; his mind was now working out a plan for tomorrow. "Do you want to have some dinner Steve? I am bloody starving. I haven't eaten all day" offered Stuart.

"No thanks Stuart, I am not really hungry, but you go ahead and I will see you later okay?"

Stuart had his usual steak for dinner along with a few glasses of merlot. He didn't drink too much for he wanted a clear head in the morning. He knew what he had to do; it was a case of do or die.

54

The next morning came quickly. Stuart had slept well. He awoke with the same sort of feeling he used to have back in Asia, just before he would go on a mission with Russell, only this time it wasn't with Russell, it was against Russell; a task that Stuart knew would test his skills to the limit.

After having a shower and dressing, Stuart went downstairs to the kitchen where he made himself two bacon rolls and a mug of coffee. It was four o'clock in the morning, and there was no one about. Stuart had a five-hour round trip ahead of him. He was going home to collect his Manlicher rifle. Knowing that Russell had the .308; Stuart didn't want to meet him unarmed. He knew that Russell would have the slight advantage over him with the .308 in the wood, as opposed to the .270. Stuart would therefore try and lure Russell out onto the open hill.

Stuart arrived at his cottage in good time. The roads had been very quiet and dry. The only stop he made on the way was to remove a mangled roe deer from the road, it must have caused considerable damage to the car that struck and killed it. There was broken glass and pieces of plastic scattered all over the road. Serves them right for going so fast, thought Stuart.

In the gun room at the cottage, Stuart took the Manlicher from the steel cabinet and gave it a clean, wiping away any excess oil and making sure each part was functioning properly. He filled the magazines and took a full box of ammunition. He felt a sudden rush of adrenalin; he was ready for the duel that lay ahead.

Stuart stopped and parked the Land Rover half a mile before he reached the big wood. He would have to use all his stalking skills and then some, for he was about to try and hunt down a skilled killer and this was the type of place the killer liked to kill. Just like in the jungle back in Asia.

Stuart skirted the edge of the big wood along the east side. The wind was coming from the west. By going this way, the deer in the wood would not pick up his scent and give his position away. He was hoping however, that they might help reveal Russell's whereabouts which would give Stuart the upper hand.

Half way up the edge of the wood, Stuart slipped into the trees and stopped. He crouched down to look and listen for any sign of movement. Nothing moved and there wasn't a sound to be heard. Slowly and carefully, Stuart crept further into the wood, stopping every five yards or so to look and listen.

Suddenly Stuart froze, for coming straight towards him were a group of stags. Their heads were bowed low, so that their antlers wouldn't touch any of the low-lying branches. Not a sound did they make. It was as if they were floating inches above the ground, weaving their way effortlessly between the trees. The mist caused by their heavy breathing, giving them a ghost-like appearance. On they came, closer. Stuart could smell them now; a strong, damp, musty odour, a smell from beyond the grave. The stags suddenly veered to the right of Stuart, no more than four yards from where he was crouched close to the ground. Holding his breath, Stuart prayed that they would keep going they did, and Stuart now knew that Russell was not far ahead, probably waiting in one of the caves, or near them.

219

For more than an hour Stuart crept slowly forward, stopping and listening every few yards. He was now fifty yards from one of the many small caves. He stopped and surveyed the scene, around the entrance to the cave were huge boulders covered in moss and scrub, growing out of these boulders were a few weedy birch trees. Stuart had used this cave once or twice in the past to shelter from a sudden downpour, he knew that the entrance was deceptive and inside the cave was quite large, high enough to stand up in and wide enough to comfortably hold five or six people. Was this the cave in which Russell is waiting?

Slowly Stuart inched his way forward taking great care not to stand on anything that would make a sound. Then heard voices from within the small cave, he lowered the rifle from his shoulder and slipped the bolt up and down, ever so quietly.

Stuart moved a few more yards further towards the cave entrance. He was now within twenty feet of the entrance. Stuart stopped and looked down at his feet. "Damn!" said Stuart quietly under his breath, for tight-up against his boot was a trip wire made from fishing gut.

55

"You took your time Stuart. Now put your rifle down." said Russell as he appeared from behind a large rock next to the cave entrance. Russell was holding Stuart's .308 rifle at waist height, the rifle was trained on Stuart. Before Stuart could regain his composure, as he had just been caught with his pants down, two men in military-style clothes emerged from the entrance.

"It's okay Stuart, we are friends." said one of the men.

"What the hell is going on?" asked Stuart.

"Come in and sit down and we will explain everything." said the other man.

Inside the cave it was quite light and spacious. There were some large rocks on the floor and Stuart noticed something else on the floor, a body bag, which appeared to have a body inside it.

"Who is that?" asked Stuart, pointing to the bag.

"That's me." said Russell with a slight grin which Stuart returned with a frown.

"Okay I am listening." said Stuart, who was still holding the manlicher, reluctant to put it down.

The unknown man began to talk "We are government agents and Russell has been working for us for some time now, in fact, since before you met him in Asia. We have been working closely with the Asian government, just as you did yourself for a few years. Our task has been to investigate multi million pound drug organisations and

find out who is at the head. Like our colleagues back in
Asia, we have now adopted their policy in that we no longer
take prisoners so we brought Russell in, to erase them"

"So where do I fit in? Is this something to do with
what happened back in Asia" asked Stuart.

"Not really, yes we certainly monitored you after you
left Asia for a year or so. We were not sure of whom else
you might have met through Richard Maynard. We also
knew that there was a strong drug connection to Scotland.
Due to the nature of our task, we could not let it be known
that the government is involved, so we let Russell loose so
to speak, leaving him to do things in his own way. I am sure
he's sorry about knocking you out and taking your rifle, but
we wanted it look like a personal vendetta and it is easier to
acquire a rifle by stealing, rather than buying one illegally
which leaves a trail and of course a government one was out
of the question." explained the Agent.

"But why kill Sharon?" asked Stuart.

"That was not our doing. The Factor obviously
thought that Sharon knew too much and had his henchmen
make it look like a hit-and-run. Russell took care of them."

"Even if the Factor had Sharon killed, but you could
have prevented her death if you had sorted out the Factor
sooner" Stuart pointed out.

"Perhaps we could have, but we had to make
absolutely sure that he was our man" reasoned the Agent.

"And what about D.S Ryan Jones, where did he fit
in?"

"Jones was just doing his job. He is a first-class
detective by the way. His superior was starting to cause
waves so we had to close the net as quickly as possible"

"Why shoot Jones?"

Russell explained "I didn't shoot Jones. He was
behind Blake and got struck in the neck by a piece of flying
bone. He'll live."

"So Russell, tell me, when I was arrested for Rick's murder and put in jail, was that part of the plan, setting me up as some sort of bait?" asked Stuart, who was stunned by the whole affair and felt rather vexed at the thought that he had been used somehow.

"No, that's just the way it happened, although once you were released from jail, I had a feeling that you might want to go home" replied Russell

"And what about you Russell? Were you in jail for two years like they say? And what about David Philips, were you really cousins?" Stuart now doubted everything he had been led to believe.

"No I was not in jail well I was for a few hours. Just long enough for the press to make a story. David Philips was an undercover Agent."

"Just how many under-cover agents are there? Or is that something that I shouldn't know about?"

"That's right Stuart, you don't need to know." said one of the Agents.

"So what happens now?" asked Stuart.

"We will now take Russell's assumed body down to where the press are waiting and then get Russell out of the country."

"And what about me, I mean why go to all this bother and explain things to me? Why involve me at all? Why not just go the way you came and no one would be any the wiser?" asked Stuart.

"Well, we would like to close the book on this, especially with D.S. Jones involved. We know from his past record that he will not give up until he was sure the case was complete. So, we are going to ask you to go along with our story. We know you can be trusted after all you didn't give Russell up even when you were in the Asian prison. Also we wonder if you would be interested in going back to work with Russell again, because we know that you are two of a kind and we have a lot of work to do. We need the best, so what do you think"

"Sure, I will go along with your story. As for your offer, no I don't think so, I am quite happy here living a quiet life." said Stuart.

Outside the cave there was a noise, a noise that Stuart was familiar with. It was the sound of a small rock hitting off a larger rock. Stuart dropped to one knee twisting around at the same time, facing the direction of the noise. As Stuart made this manoeuvre he brought his rifle to his shoulder, in one easy action, looking for the target.

"It's good to see that you haven't lost your touch Stuart" said Russell, who like the two agents, wasn't unduly concerned about the sound from outside the cave. Stuart remained in his position for a few seconds, and then rose to his feet, shouldering his rifle. He felt slightly embarrassed about his reaction, as he realised how stupid he must have looked. Stuart had no sooner stood up when the figure of a man appeared at the entrance of the cave.

Stuart got the shock of his life, not so much at the sudden appearance of the man, rather at who he was.

"Bloody hell! I thought you were killed in Asia." said Stuart, as he took a step backwards.

"Hello Stuart, sorry to startle you like this."

"Okay, does someone want to tell me what the fuck is going on here?"

"Stuart I would like you to meet Captain Philip Jameson, our co-ordinator in all of our operations." said one of the Agents. Stuart shook his head.

"I don't believe you guys! So tell me, Captain Philip Jameson, if of course that's your real name, because the last time that we met it was David Philips, who as it happens, was supposedly killed. Why fake your own death?"

"My cover was about to be blown, so I had to disappear quickly and so did the two guys that were onto me."

"So you had Russell here take care of them, right?"

"That's right Mr Brodie, as you know the line of business that we are in is very much a case of do, or die. Not only am I the co-ordinator in all of the operations, I am also the path-finder, or the front man if you like. My job is to go into the enemy's zone and as you know, the enemy at the present are drug dealers. It's the big fish that we are after, the ones that normally walk away at the end of the day to start up again. We find out who they are and how they operate. Nothing is left to chance, so that when it is time for the hit, or in this case hits, Russell has all of the information that he needs, right down to the last detail and I monitor him all of the time."

"So you witness all of the killings then?" asked Stuart still bemused.

"More or less and if during an operation I see that something isn't going as planned, then I can stop it at anytime" explained Captain Jameson.

"What about the elusive Dr Russell, where does he fit in? I am pretty sure that he does, somewhere along the line."

"I am, or I should say was, Dr Russell" replied Captain Jameson with a smile.

"Well now, isn't that a surprise, but why use the name Russell? Surely you must have realised that it would bring you under suspicion?" Stuart was genuinely surprised this was the last thing he had expected that Dr Russell would turn out to be a dead man.

"It was meant to Mr Brodie, for two reasons. First, I knew that once you found out about me, you would speak to your Factor. I had to make sure that I knew who all of the players were. We have been particularly suspicious of the estate owners the Bellinghams. We checked them out but could find no link. It seems that it actually was just a coincidence that they bought the estate. I used their names to test if the Factor would make contact with them but he didn't and that was extra assurance that the Bellinghams are not involved."

"You said for two reasons. What was the second?"

"The second reason was you Mr Brodie."

"You wanted to see if I would panic at the thought of Russell staying under the same roof, is that it?" guessed Stuart perceptively.

"That's right Mr Brodie and I was glad to see that you didn't."

"But why? I knew that Russell was already playing at silly-buggers with me."

"Do you remember in Asia when you first met Russell?"

"Yes, go on."

"Well, Russell saw great potential in you and he was right, you worked well together. I was there remember and you now know what my job is. I monitored you all the time you were in Asia and even back then I knew that drug trail lead to Scotland and I thought that you could possibly take care of things here for us" elaborated Captain Jameson.

"If you are in control did you set me up for Rick's murder back in Asia and even had me sent to jail?" said Stuart he was beginning to piece it together.

"Yes, sorry about that Mr Brodie, but it was a big part of your training" said Captain Philips.

"What! To see if I would crack?" Stuart was a bit annoyed.

"It wasn't so much to see if you would crack, it was more a lesson for you, to ensure that you would be careful in the future and I am quite sure that it worked, in fact I bet that you told yourself that you would never go to jail again?"

"You certainly got that one right" admitted Stuart.

"Having you arrested and sent to jail, I also got you out again remember, was also a good excuse to get you out of the country and back here where we needed you" continued Captain Jameson.

"So what went wrong with your plans for me?"

"Nothing and there still isn't. It was merely the fact that there were too many players involved. I did think about linking you up with Russell again, but when we discovered that your Factor was the top man, I decided to monitor you instead and see how you coped" explained Captain Jameson.

"So it has been you that has been spying on me? Testing me? And all the time I thought that it was Russell" this was making sense to Stuart, if it had been Russell Stuart never would have spotted him.

"Yes I have been Mr Brodie and even after today I am happy to say that you have definitely got what it takes"

"Definitely got what it takes to do what? Become a killer?"

"You have done it before remember."

"That's all in the past, a long time ago and there's no way that I will go back" asserted Stuart.

"Look Mr Brodie, I don't need a commitment from you right now. What I will do is give you a telephone number to call. If you decide to come on board, you can call the number day or night and we will take it from there, okay?"

"Okay, but my answer right now, is no" it was all too much for Stuart to think about at the moment.

The Captain's mobile phone rang. He answered it straight away, Stuart could just make out the callers voice it was a man voice with a strong American accent, but he couldn't make out what was being said. The Captain strolled out of the cave saying very little into the mobile. Stuart strained to hear a few words before the Captain was out of ear shot, "Yes, everything is complete. Yes, he will be there in a day or so."

The Captain returned "Okay, well look, here is that number Mr Brodie. Call if you should change your mind and thanks"

The two Agents started off down through the wood dragging Russell's so-called body. They also took Stuart's .308 rifle with them. Stuart realised that he wouldn't see that again, not that he particularly wanted the rifle back knowing that it had been used to murder his boss and the head of Glasgow Police. Captain Philip Jameson, if that was his real name, followed on behind.

Stuart and Russell sat and chatted for a while, "Sorry I shot one of your deer, but we needed a body to complete the scenario. In fact, it's a pity that we had to meet under these circumstances and if you do change your mind, I would be happy to have you tag along." said Russell.

"That's not for me any more Russell and by the way, I owe you one." said Stuart rubbing the side of his neck.

"Perhaps some day, old pal." said Russell with a grin, as he slipped away into the wood just like one of the stags, the ghosts in the wood. Stuart wondered if he would ever see him again; maybe in hell.

On the evening news it was reported that a crazed killer, after an extensive manhunt, had been shot dead in a remote wood, sixty miles north of Glasgow. His motive apparently for the brutal murders, which had started in Asia, then moved to London and ended in Scotland, was that he had become a vigilante after his cousin had been murdered by members of a drug ring. The drug ring no longer existed.

56

Stuart arrived at the hospital in the late afternoon. It was the same hospital where he had been treated himself the day before. Stuart walked over to the reception. The same pretty young nurse was behind the desk, the one that Steve had taken a shine to.

"Hello Mr Brodie, I didn't expect to see you again so soon"

"Hi, and I certainly didn't expect to be back so soon either."

"So what can I do for you today Mr Brodie?"

"Well I was actually hoping to see Ryan Jones."

"Okay, just let me check."

Stuart listened to her telephone conversation. He was glad at what he over heard. Ryan was now out of intensive care and it would be alright for him to go and see Ryan.

"You can go and see Mr Jones. He is in room three, ward five."

"Thanks, and by the way you made quite an impression on Steve the other day" said Stuart with a smile. The young nurse blushed slightly as she returned the smile.

"So did he, I have to admit"

"I can detect the start of a budding romance here."

"Perhaps, you can never tell Mr Brodie."

"Well all I can say is you won't meet a nicer guy than Steve. Good luck to you both"

"Yes he certainly seems a nice person. I am meeting him at the weekend and thanks."

Stuart gave the young nurse a smile and headed towards the lift, thinking to himself on the way, Steve hadn't wasted any time. Love at first sight indeed! It was time the big bugger settled down anyway and he was right about what he told the young nurse. She wouldn't meet a nicer guy and for him like-wise, for she seemed like a very pleasant girl.

Ryan was propped up in bed with several pillows. His eyes were closed and he looked fast asleep. Stuart wasn't sure whether to wake him or not.

"Can I come in?" asked Stuart quietly.
Ryan's eyes opened. He focused on Stuart and beckoned with his left hand for him to come in. Stuart noticed the intravenous drip going to his other arm and the dressing covering the wound on Ryan's neck.

"How are you feeling Ryan?"

"Never felt better. Great stuff morphine." said Ryan in a husky low voice.

"If you want I can come back later."

"No I am fine honestly. You'll just have to excuse my voice and the fact that I am still a bit dopey. They operated on my neck early this morning. They removed a large chunk of bone, part of Blake's rib cage apparently. It was lodged between two vertebrae. They tell me I am lucky, for if it had gone another few millimetres, it would have severed my spinal cord. I call it unlucky. So tell me Stuart if you can, what the fuck happened?"

"No one's told you?"

"No, I have only been properly awake for a few hours."

"Well, it seems Russell blew the Factor's head off and shot Blake in the chest. Unfortunately, you were behind her. Christine apparently witnessed the whole thing. She's in another ward recovering from shock. I will pop in and see her later."

"And what about Hodges, any sign of him?"

"He's dead. He was shot by some special police unit or other."

"Thank God for that. So it's all over"

"Yes. I don't know what will happen on the estate. I suppose we'll find out soon enough. I imagine that you will be glad to get back to London."

"Not really, I think I might take early retirement after this. Maybe I will buy a small cottage up here."

"That's a good idea Ryan I could do with an assistant"

"I might just take you up on that Stuart."

Stuart could see that Ryan was beginning to flag a little.

"Listen Ryan, I am going to pop along and see how Christine's doing before it gets too late. I will look back in before I go, if that's okay"

"Sure Stuart, on you go I will see you later."

Stuart went and saw Christine, but unfortunately, she was in no fit state to make conversation. She was still in a state of shock and obviously quite heavily sedated. Stuart didn't sit with her for long but he did promise her that he would come back and visit her when she felt better. Stuart felt really sorry for her lying there, with a blank expression on her withered and tired-looking face, especially as she had no family whatsoever, although she had plenty of friends in the village. Surely some of them would come and visit her. When Stuart returned to Ryan's room, Ryan was fast asleep.

"Sleep well my friend." Stuart said, in a caring way. He once again cursed Russell, not about the murders that Russell had committed, more but the suffering that he had caused to the innocent.

There was poor old Christine, who would probably never be the same again after her ordeal. Then there was

Ryan, who as it turned out, was lucky to be alive. Luckily Russell's mission was over and now everyone could get on with their lives again; well the ones that still had a life.

Stuart couldn't completely condemn Russell for his actions as he understood Russell's purpose in life. After all he had been Russell's right hand man for several years, participating in the deadly games. Deep down, Stuart had an admiration for the guy. It was just a pity about the innocent bystanders this time, for normally there wouldn't be any, or at least none that Stuart knew about. Shit happens from time to time and we can't see around the corners.

57

Russell sat at an airport bar sipping coffee. The woman who approached him was smartly dressed, in her mid thirties and very attractive.

"Hello Russell"

"Hi Jill, you are looking smart as usual. Can I get you a drink?"

"No thanks Russell, I don't have long, my plane takes off in half an hour"

"Where are you off to this time Jill?"

"Back to Asia I'm afraid. I managed to get the name of Maynard's replacement from the Factor, so it's back to work and if all goes well, we might see you back there." She replied

"Yes I hope so because I rather miss the place" said Russell.

"Where are you heading?" asked Jill.

"Canada as if you didn't know" replied Russell.

"Well someone has to line up the targets for you, and I didn't spend two months in Canada for nothing. I gather that your old side-kick doesn't want to come back on board?"

"No unfortunately, well not at the moment anyway."

"That's a pity, because I would quite like to get to know him" responded Jill with a wicked smile.

"Oh you would, would you?" laughed Russell.

"Yes, he kind of reminds me of you" Jill laughed and looked for a response, Russell raised an eyebrow. Jill sighed "Well, I better get going or I will miss my flight. Goodbye Russell, and take care." Jill leant over and gave Russell a hug and a kiss on the check.

"Yes I will and you too. Goodbye Jill."

Russell's gaze followed Jill as she left the bar. Smiling, he couldn't help but admire the woman. She was as much a professional as he was and he liked to work with professionals.

The man sitting two seats behind Russell was also smiling. He had overheard the conversation and was glad his team got on so well together.

Epilogue

Ryan was highly commended for his part in bringing the biggest drug ring in the U.K to an end. He accepted the offer of promotion to Inspector even though he didn't relish the thought of being office bound and was even contemplating early retirement.

Although the Bellingham's had not been involved in any way whatsoever, they found the scandal about the estate all too much. They decided to sell the estate, which was snapped up very quickly by a rich business man. Stuart carried on working on the estate under a new Factor, who was appointed by the new owner.

Stuart kept in touch with Ryan who said that he would come up and see him once he had fully recovered. He also told Stuart that he might even buy a small cottage in Scotland to live in when he retired.

Whenever Stuart heard something on the news about victims of drug-related deaths, he would take the small piece of paper from under the clock on the mantelpiece. He would look hard at the telephone number written on it and think that maybe he should put his talent to better use.

Please turn the page for a preview of Ronald Findlay's

Bagpipes and Blood

A Stuart Brodie Novel

Due for release in June 2008.

www.lulu.com

1

The overhanging crag provided excellent shade against the blazing sun. It hadn't rained for over two months now. It was a scorching heat, the hottest summer recorded in fifty years, rivers and lochs were at an all time low.

Stuart gazed across the moor the horizon was a blur due to the rising heat waves. The peat bogs, like the waterways had all but dried up. The surfaces of the bogs had turned into craters with a hard baked crust. It was one of these peat bogs that drew Stuart's attention gathered around it were a group of Hooded crows. The crows were arguably fighting over something that was rich in their picking, tasty enough to keep them out in the blazing afternoon sun. Hooded crows normally do their scavenging at dusk and dawn.

After a while, curiosity got the better of Stuart, he left the shade of the overhanging crag and started making his way down to the crows. Stuart avoided stepping into the bogs even although their hard baked surfaces looked solid it was hard to tell what weight they would support. Stuart knew only too well the dangers of the peat bogs some of them were bottomless pits. Similar to quick sand, if you fell into one it was hard to get out, impossible even.

Stuart was about two hundred yards from the crows, it was only then that they took to the air. They were obviously reluctant to leave their tasty meal; normally you couldn't get within five hundred yards of these wily birds. A tasty meal indeed, thought Stuart as he got a whiff of rotten flesh. When Stuart arrived at the food source, it didn't take him long to realise what it was that the crows had been feeding on. What lay before Stuart was a grisly sight indeed, protruding through the hard baked surface of the peat bog was a human head, or rather, what was left of it. The side that was visible had almost been stripped to the bone. Where the right ear had been there was now a stinking hole, and where the right eye once was, an empty socket. The crows, in their greed had managed to dislodge some of the teeth; they lay discarded on the hard surface of the peat. The hooded crows had no respect for the dead, to them, a meal was a meal.

Stuart stared down at the gruesome discovery, what should he do? He could just walk away and forget all about it, but he should allow the body some respect, and report it? He really didn't want to get involved, especially not with his past, not to mention that the folk still hadn't forgotten his last escapade, only two years ago, which ended up with several people dead.

Stuart covered the head as best he could; he pulled up large handfuls of dried sphagnum moss and what heather he could find, and placed it over the head. He hoped that this would deter the crows for a while and any other scavengers that might be drawn to it by the smell.

On his way back across the moor to where his Land Rover was parked. Stuart wondered about the head in the bog. Who was it? How long had it been there? Was it male or female? The crows had done quite a number on the head, making it impossible to tell. The hair that had been visible was caked with hard, dried up peat. Was it some poor unsuspecting hill walker who had got lost in the mist, and stumbled into the bog, or was it something more sinister than that? Stuart would like to investigate but that could lead to a lot of trouble, just like last time. He decided to wait until he got off the hill before deciding what to do.

Stuart drove up a winding driveway, at the top of which was a quaint, but handsome cottage. Blocking the driveway was a wheelbarrow, Stuart got out of the Land Rover to move it and then he noticed the gardener hard at work in the rose bed.

"Hello Stuart, how are you? I haven't seen you in a while"

"Hi Ryan, it's good to see you hard at work"

"Indeed, but I think I'm wasting my time, this bloody heat is killing everything, especially since they introduced the hose pipe ban"

"Tell me about it. Is there any chance of a cuppa?"

"Of course there is old boy, come on in out of the heat."

"Thanks very much."

"So what brings you in today? Just passing by?"

"Well no, not quite, I've got something I wanted to run past you."

"Go on" urged Ryan wondering at Stuart's reluctance.

"I was out on the hill today; I was sheltering under the crag out of the sun. I noticed a group of hooded crows out in the peat bogs. It's not like them to be out in the scorching heat and it made me a little wary as they were fighting like hell with each other over something. I wanted to know what had gotten them so crazy, but I certainly didn't expect it to be what it was"

"What was it?" asked Ryan

"A human head, submerged in a bog, only half is visible, the rest, I assume, is still attached to a body"

"Bloody hell Stuart are you sure it's human?" exclaimed Ryan

"I am quite sure Ryan it's a human head alright"

"Have you got any idea who it might be?"

"No none at all there's not much left; the Crows have all but stripped it to the bone. In fact I can't tell whether it's a man or a woman"

"Christ, you must have got one hell of a shock when you realised what it was"

"Not really, I have seen many a gruesome sight over the years I was more surprised than anything"

"I take it that you have informed the local police about it?"

"Not yet, I thought I would speak to you about it first, seeing as how you are a great detective and all that" Stuart cajoled with a smile.

The smile wasn't returned by Ryan.

"I was in two minds to bury it and forget all about it" continued Stuart.

"You didn't bury it did you?"

"No, I 'm curious to know who it is"

"Thanks for the consideration Stuart, but as you know I'm retired"

"Come on Ryan, once a policeman, always a policeman, isn't that true? And don't tell me that you're not interested?"

"That maybe so, but you still have to inform the local police, the sooner the better I would say"

"Yes I suppose you're right, I covered the head up with moss by the way"

"Good" said Ryan with a slight smile.

Stuart called the local police and informed them of his grisly find, he pointed out to the policeman that due to the time of day, it would be getting dark soon and it could be dangerous trekking through the bogs even though they appeared dry. So between them they decided it would be best if they waited until the morning. They arranged to meet at six am at the foot of the hill road that led to the moor. Stuart would take them to the spot where he found the head.

The policeman asked Stuart to keep the find to himself for the time being.

Stuart stayed at Ryan's cottage for another hour, discussing who the head in the bog might belong to, and how it came to be there. Just as Stuart was preparing to leave, Ryan received a phone call from the local policeman, who Ryan had got to know quite well over the last year or so. The policeman told Ryan briefly about the conversation that he'd had with Stuart Ryan pretended to be surprised at the news of the head in the bog.

After finishing up the call Ryan turned to Stuart "Looks like I'll be joining you in the morning for the uncovering of the head. Best not let on that we spoke already"

"Don't worry, I won't. Retired eh? I think that you're about to be re-instated"

"Well I don't know about that, let's wait and see"

N